Judith dissolved into tears....

Her heart was broken. She had stood at her window and watched as the one and only man for her smiled, tipped his hat, then went out of her life forever.

Her family was certain she would forget all about him, that her upcoming social season in London society would deliver up many suitors—one of whom was bound to catch her fancy.

But her family had not counted on Judith's determination; on her undaunted trust in an uncertain future....

These titles may be available at your local bookstore.

Heir Presumptive

PATRICIA ORMSBY

A MASQUERADE HISTORICAL FROM

W🌐RLDWIDE

TORONTO • LONDON • NEW YORK

For Gay and
my other good friends
in Essex

Masquerade Historical edition published March 1980
ISBN 0-373-74536-2

Originally published in 1978
by Peter Davies Limited

Printed in Canada

CHAPTER
ONE

THE occasion was the first notable sale of the year at Tattersall's. A bright sun lent colour to the animated scene as Mr Richard Tattersall, who had taken over the conduct of the firm since the death of his father the previous year, limped across the enclosure and mounted the rostrum. The stable clock struck twelve as he tapped lightly with his gavel for silence and, looking about him, he was gratified to perceive that many gentlemen of consequence were to be observed among the chattering throng. Pinks of the Swells, Tulips of the Goes, fox-hunting clericals, knowing horse-dealers, loungers and sporting men of all descriptions were crowded into the famous Yard. Indeed, so close-packed was the assembly that many were obliged to stand in the passage outside the covered gateway, while a number, despairing of getting to within earshot of the auctioneer, were strolling about on the gravel path that bordered the green lawn. In the midst of all this activity, the effigy of the Fox sat sedately beneath his dome that sheltered the pump in the centre of the Yard.

'It is said that Nairn is putting his entire stables under the hammer,' remarked Mr Scrope Davies to his companion as the hubbub around him died down and the first of the horses offered was led into the Yard.

Lord Penston shrugged his broad shoulders, impeccably encased in a coat of blue Bath cloth. 'Depend on it, his latest Bird of Paradise is proving expensive,' he answered curtly.

'Oh, who has he in keeping now?'

'Some French filly, I understand, but Creevey would be better placed to inform you on that head. I have not exchanged words with Rollo Nairn these five years.'

'He lives for the most part in Brussels, does he not?'

Penston took out his snuff-box and helped himself with a neat turn of the wrist. 'Did he live in the next house to me, I can assure you that the circumstances would not be other than they are,' he remarked coldly.

Davies smiled. 'Hardly a friend of Rollo's, were you, Guy?' he murmured.

'Not unless you count being in love with his wife an earnest of friendship!' retorted the other with perfect candour.

'Nonsense! You were only a child.'

'Just turned nineteen and she a year older. Which is why her parents would have none of me.'

'And she?'

'Accepted my devotion with an easy grace.' A wry smile touched Penston's fine mouth. 'Her page, she called me, and I was well content merely to breathe the air she moved through, to touch the things her hand had rested on. Then Rollo Nairn, less nice than I, appeared on the scene and bore her off like the swashbuckling pirate he is. What a fool a young man in love is to be sure.'

'Nairn was also ten years your senior and a deal more than that in worldly wisdom, I'd say,' mused Davies. 'You are godfather to the boy, are you not?'

'Yes. His father did not care too much for that so, since Mary's death, I have not set eyes on the lad. Rollo holds no better opinion of me than I of him.'

Davies said no more on the subject, but his eyes rested thoughtfully on his friend's handsome person which was, as he well knew, allied to an equally handsome fortune, and he could not but reflect that it was close on seven years since Sir Rollo had been made a widower yet Penston had shown no urge to replace the lady in his affections nor to seek a wife. Now none but the most hopeful of mamas could dream of ensnaring so hardened a bachelor.

Unconscious of his friend's scrutiny, Penston tipped his tall-crowned hat a little to one side of his head, revealing thick fair hair as yet untinged with grey despite his forty years and, raising his quizzing-glass, allowed his cool gaze to range over the colourful assembly.

Just then a hand brushed his sleeve and he became aware of a small, stout, agitated personage at his elbow, who seemed bent on claiming his attention.

'Who the devil — why, to be sure, it is Ned Walters! This is a sad day for you, my old friend.'

'Sadder than you can imagine, Mr Guy — I mean, my lord,' replied Sir Rollo Nairn's agent, touching the brim of his hat. 'I am more than happy to see you here, I can tell you. I had thought you to be still in the Peninsula.'

'I sold out when my father died — did not the Gaffer tell you?'

Mr Walters grimaced at mention of his venerable sire, agent for many years to Lord Penston's father. 'A brief message, as is his custom, to tell me of his lordship's passing. I was much grieved to hear it. A fine gentleman and ever a good friend to me.'

Lord Penston looked down on the little man with a speculative gleam in his eye. 'What troubles you, Ned?' he asked.

Mr Walters glanced apologetically at Mr Davies who, taking the hint, moved a little away. 'Sir — my lord, you are Mr Rodney's godfather — oh, I know it's little you've seen of him since her ladyship died, rest her sweet soul, but he is not yet of age and there is no one else I can turn to.'

Lord Penston looked his astonishment. 'Surely her ladyship's family —' he began.

'They have been so disgusted by Sir Rollo's conduct that they have ceased to acknowledge him or the boy. As for the Nairns, the few that survive live in outlandish parts of Scotland and would not hold the matter to be any of their concern. My lord, the entire stable is to be sold, including Mr Rodney's own horses — even The Centaur that you sent him for his eighteenth birthday.'

'What? He has no right!'

'That's my opinion, my lord, but it is a magnificent beast and could fetch a high price.'

'I'll speak to Mr Tattersall. It must be withdrawn.'

'Thank you, my lord. There's another thing, Sir Rollo wants not less than twenty thousand pounds from this sale, all to be sent to him. There's no provision for his son.'

'Is the boy here?'

'If you will step back a pace, my lord, and look to that corner, you may see him.'

An involuntary gasp escaped Penston as his eyes sought out and rested on the tall, slim young gentleman standing with folded arms and sternly composed countenance at the back of the eager throng.

'By Jupiter, he is as like to his mother as he can stare!' he muttered, plainly moved by this jolt to his memory.

'Will you have a word with him, my lord? The poor lad is well nigh desperate. The stable was all he had, y'see. He is talking of enlisting as a common soldier.'

'Has he no money of his own?'

'A pittance from his mother only. His father paid him an allowance to look after the stable when he came away from Rugby School — as head groom, you might say, but that will cease now. Since the lad grew to manhood, they have ever been by the ears.'

'Let me see, his birthday is this coming month, he'll be twenty, I do declare. Great Heaven, how the years fly past!'

'Aye, my lord. We are both of an age to think on't now.'

As if sensing their attention, the young man turned his head and looked in their direction. Once again the remembrance of his beautiful mother tugged at Lord Penston's heart as he met the despairing regard of those black-lashed grey eyes, set beneath wide-arching brows. For a moment no gleam of recognition was apparent in the lad's gaze, which was not to be wondered at for he had not seen his godfather since his thirteenth birthday, then an expression of the purest delight lit up his countenance and his lips parted in a tentative smile.

'I'll go to him. Be so good as to wait upon me at my house after the sale, Ned.'

'Uncle Guy!' Rodney Nairn advanced to greet him as speedily as the press of people would allow, both hands outstretched in eager welcome. 'It *is* you! I — I am not dreaming?'

'It is I. Though I'd say you were more like to be in a nightmare than a dream, my poor child. Why, in God's name, did you not apply to me?'

'It is The Centaur,' said the boy in a distracted tone. 'I cannot bear for him to be sold.'

'He shall not be. Stay here while I have a word with Richard Tattersall.'

Easily, without apparent effort, his lordship moved through the dense gathering; a smile here, a touch there, and the tight ranks parted to allow his passage. He was checked for a moment by Lord Derby, who asked his opinion on the hunter being paraded and then, that sale completed, he stepped up to the rostrum. Mr Tattersall courteously inclined his head to hear what he had to say before continuing with the group.

'You have a horse here, Richard, that is not yours to sell, a half-Arab, named Centaur. I sent him home from the Peninsula to my godson, Mr Rodney Nairn, to keep in his charge until I should return to claim him.'

Mr Tattersall's pleasing countenance clouded over. 'Forgive me, my lord, but have you proof of this?'

'None but my word. If it puts you in a difficulty with your client, let the horse be offered and I will match the highest bidder.'

Mr Tattersall, though but twenty-six years of age was, like all his family, as shrewd a judge of character as of horseflesh.

'There will be no need for that,' he said at once. 'I will give instructions for The Centaur to be taken to your stables after the sale. Could you, my lord, write to Sir Rollo and explain that he was under a misapprehension in supposing the beast to be his own?' Their eyes met momentarily and then Mr Tattersall's ready smile provoked a responsive quirk of the lips from Penston. 'Pray, Richard, do not be at outs with Sir Rollo over this. I will bear the blame if he gets on his high ropes.'

With a nod he walked away and made a leisurely return to Mr Nairn's side. The boy looked at him in eager question.

'You have arranged something, sir?'

'You will be so good as to remember, Rodney, that I gave The Centaur into your keeping until I should return to England — oh, yes, after close on two years you have come to think of yourself as the owner of the animal, but you are not, you know.'

Rodney grinned appreciatively. 'Nor, through me, is my

father! Thank you, sir,' he said, and then sighed. 'I wish to God all my troubles were so easily resolved.'

'I cannot imagine,' said his godfather, looking about him, 'that you are enjoying any moment of this. If you would be so good as to accompany me to my house in Arlington Street then, perhaps, I may learn precisely what has been happening to you in the past six or seven years and in what manner I may be of service to you now.' Seeing the boy's hesitation, he added, 'Ned Walters will be visiting me after the sale. You may learn all the details from him without enduring the misery of watching your horses come under the hammer.'

Half-an-hour later saw the two gentlemen comfortably seated on either side of a welcoming fire in the book-room of Lord Penston's modish establishment in Arlington Street, partaking of what his lordship was pleased to describe as a very tolerable Madeira. As he discoursed pleasantly on various topics, putting the lad at his ease, he was gratified to observe that, while not precisely cutting a swell, his godson presented a very genteel appearance in buff kerseymere pantaloons, striped toilinette waistcoat, half-boots, and a coat of superfine which, if it had not been fashioned by one of the great artists of the day, at least lost nothing in the wearing, for young Mr Nairn was blessed with a pair of shoulders and a waist that had no need of artificial aids. Indeed his whole form displayed a well-made elegance most pleasing to the eye, and had it not been for his rather drawn and anxious expression his good looks must have been considered quit unexceptionable. Lord Penston judged him to be a shy young man, at home to a peg where horseflesh was concerned, but in worldly matters a mere pigeon for the plucking.

'Sir — Uncle Guy,' he began diffidently, as if uncertain of how he should address his godfather.

'Not "Uncle Guy", I think,' remarked the latter gentleman pensively. 'So very ageing, don't you agree? I thank God I have no nephews or nieces! Now, I am given to understand by Ned Walters that you have the intention of enlisting as a common soldier. Would not a commission be more comfortable?'

The boy flushed to the roots of his dark hair, but answered in a perfectly composed manner. 'Infinitely, sir, but a pair of colours costs money and I — I have none, or very little.'

'Your father?'

'Will grant me an allowance if I carry out his wishes. But if I do carry out his wishes then I am unlikely to enter the army.'

'I see,' Lord Penston twirled the wineglass in his long fingers, watching the firelight reflect off the amber liquid. 'And your father's wishes are — ?'

'That I pay my addresses to a certain young lady and, when her father's consent is obtained, marry her. That is why I am so — so fashionably attired. My father's instructions were that I should see to the sale of his horses and then present myself to the lady's father with no loss of time.'

'Surely,' said his godfather gently, 'you are a shade young to be thinking of setting up your nursery?'

'There is no immediate question of that, sir.' The devil! thought Penston, the poor lad will take fire if he blushes any deeper! 'The young lady is but sixteen. Her parent — she has no mother — does not wish her to marry for at least a year. But my father is desirous of contracting me to her as soon as possible.'

'Why, is she an heiress?'

'A very considerable one, I believe. Her father, a Mr George Hammerton, is something in the City, concerned with trade. I do not know precisely what his business is.'

'And he would buy a title for his daughter, is that it?'

'He is wishful of launching her into society and would be in a better way to succeed were she Mrs Rodney Nairn rather than Miss Judith Hammerton.'

'Hmm. But why you, if she is so considerable an heiress? Oh, mistake me not, your birth and standing are of the best, but there are many titled sprigs of greater consequence who would be prepared to accept a Cit for a father-in-law if he undertook to rescue 'em from the River Tick.'

'I — I am very likely to be calling myself Viscount Quendon one day.'

'What? Has Quendon lost both his sons, then?'

'Yes, the younger just lately, I believe. And his second wife has produced him only a daughter.'

'So your father is his heir? I'll allow that puts a different complexion on affairs for I would hazard a guess that Quendon is past sixty. Who is his second wife?'

'An old childhood friend and a widow of some years when he married her. She is not likely to be presenting him with further proofs of her affection.'

The bitterness in the young voice caused Penston to rise quickly and refill their glasses. 'Now, do not be thinking yourself a sacrifice on the altar of your father's gaming debts,' he said kindly. 'This sort of arrangement is not uncommon, you know. For the lady's part, a good introduction to society must be considered a desideratum while, for you, such a marriage spells independence.'

'Say, rather, the exchange of one set of shackles for another!' burst out Rodney. 'I'll not live on my wife.'

'It is possible that your father-in-law might agree with you there,' commented Penston drily as he set down the decanter. 'I must confess, however, that I had not suspected Sir Rollo of being so considerate of your future. Most commendable in so ramshackle a parent!'

'You may rest easy on that score, sir!' the lad flashed back. 'Depend upon it, he has thought only for how *he* may profit by such an arrangement. My welfare is hardly a first consideration with him. I — I serve only as a reminder to him of my mother.' Seeing his godfather's look of enquiry he went on more quietly. 'She — she grew to hate him, I do believe, though she was at pains to conceal her aversion, at least before me.'

Lord Penston made no attempt to hide his astonishment. 'I had no notion that such a poor understanding existed between your parents. It was not ever thus, I can assure you.'

He paused, thinking back over the past, then he went on in a brisk tone, 'If you are set on entering the army, it will be very much more agreeable for us both if you were to take a commission in a sound cavalry regiment. I can arrange that for you in no time at all.'

'But — my father?' objected Rodney, looking bewildered, as well he might, at this neat disposition of his future.

'Need not know yet awhile. When he does, it could prove a

costly and elaborate business to extricate you. I doubt he will put himself to so much trouble. As I see it, our first obstacle is Mr Hammerton. How far are you committed in this affair, do you know?'

'I am persuaded by the tone of my father's letter that I have but to present myself and unless either Mr Hammerton or his daughter takes me in strong aversion, or I show myself to be quite ineligible in some way, I — I am at liberty to pay my addresses to the young lady. It — it seems a trifle odd to me, sir.'

Recalling Rollo Nairn's top-lofty condescension towards the 'middling class', it seemed a trifle odd to Lord Penston also, but he merely nodded and said: 'How much does Ned Walters know of this?'

'I imagine all of it, sir, though we have discussed it very little, it all being of so recent a nature.'

'Then I think it best to do nothing until he presents himself here.' His lordship glanced at his watch. 'It is long past the hour for nuncheon but I find myself remarkably sharp-set. Will you join me in a light refreshment?' He stepped to the bell-pull and his summons was presently answered by his butler, a spare elderly man, of impassive mien and stately bearing. 'Ah, Bairstow! Mr Nairn and I find the prospect of fasting until dinner time rather beyond our powers. Can you tempt us with some confection of Raoul's contriving?'

'Indeed, my lord, not having understood that you were to set out so early this morning, he has prepared a Périgord pie with truffles, such as your lordship is very partial to, together with some oyster patties. There is also a cold fowl —'

Lord Penston checked this recital with upraised hand. 'Enough!' he pleaded. 'It seems we shall do very well. And, I think, the champagne, Bairstow.'

When the butler had withdrawn to carry out his master's wishes, Rodney said, a little anxiously, 'I must return to Lambourne, sir, for my father has charged me with paying off the stable staff and — and putting the house in order to receive a visit from my future wife.'

Lord Penston waved away his objections. 'Walters can see to that. I shall require you to be with me to-morrow in any case.

When you have eaten you will go and leave your card at Mr Hammerton's house. He, at least, must entertain no suspicion of your intentions lest word gets to your father's ears before we can make our arrangements.'

'But sir, the young lady —' protested Rodney. 'Will it not seem — well, discourteous, to say the least, to offer to pay my addresses to her and then to take myself off without a word of explanation?'

Lord Penston glanced at him keenly. 'Have you seen her yet? Is she well-favoured?'

'I have no notion of what she may be like.'

'Then since the affections are in no way engaged, I fancy we need not entertain any fears that the lady will fall into a decline.'

His godfather's dry tone prompted Rodney to answer spiritedly. 'Maybe not, sir, but will she not have the right to feel slighted and her father to consider that I have behaved in a very ungentlemanlike way?'

'I cannot conceive how he should be setting himslf up as a judge of any such thing, but I fancy a courteous letter of explanation when you are established in your new career will meet the case.'

As it was plain that Lord Penston held no good opinion of Cits who aimed to use their money-bags to ease themselves into society, Rodney said no more but applied himself to the excellent meal that was presently set before him with an appetite that did not appear to be in the least impaired by the weight of trouble upon his shoulders. Conversation flowed easily between them for the boy was all eagerness to learn of his godfather's exploits as a Colonel of Hussars in the Peninsula. For his part, Penston was content to answer the flood of questions, slipping in one here and there himself so that he was very soon in possession of all the relevant facts appertaining to his godson's life since leaving Rugby School. So absorbed were they in each other's company that the sound of the bracket clock, set on a stand by the window, striking the hour of four quite dismayed his lordship.

'Good God! You had best take yourself off. We will have Ned Walters with us within the hour. Where is Mr Hammerton lodged?'

'He has taken the lease of a house in Bury Street, at No. 26, so I understand.'

'A neighbour of Tom Moore's, is he? An odd circumstance for a city man to be setting himself down amid the literary lions. It is only a step from here but Mr Hammerton may well hold to the old style of dining early and will not be best pleased to receive his future son-in-law with a napkin tucked into his waistcoat.'

Rodney flushed again at his godfather's way of speaking of his proposed wife's father. 'He — he may not be quite so Gothic in his ways as you suppose, sir. His lady, I understand, was of a good family, though I fancy they cast her off when she married him.'

'Which, I dare say, would account for his wishing to establish his daughter as high as is in his power. Let me look at you. Yes, you will do very well. That Brutus cut is just the thing for young fellows of your stamp, though it is not to my style at all. Now, remember, if you please, no word of your true intentions. You are fulfilling your father's instructions to call upon Mr Hammerton. Allow him to do the talking.'

*   *   *

After Rodney had left him, Lord Penston sat down again by the fire and gave himself up to serious thought. To have cherished a hopeless passion for more than twenty years for a lady who had been, to his belief, happily married for much of that time was, he was willing to admit, coming it rather too strong. As a young man he had set Mary Nairn upon a pedestal far above the common touch, but by his thirtieth year he had long come to terms with so unrewarding a devotion and had formed as many discreet connections as any other young blood of his day. But it pleased him to enact the rôle of *cavaliere servente* as it amused her to accept his chivalrous homage, and when she died he had grieved deeply and sincerely as he would for the loss of a dear friend. Her husband's latent but enduring antagonism had served to keep the fire smouldering on his part at least, though Mary had always made it clear he could never supersede Rollo in her affections nor provoke her to infidelity. And if the beau monde had shaken its collective head and whispered knowingly of a broken heart when he had left the world of fashion for the sterner one of war, who was he to deny them their conjecture? Though, truth to tell, it had been boredom rather than the dictates of unfulfilled passion that had governed his actions. Of latter years, Mary's image had all but faded from his mind until that very day when the sight of her son had so sharply revived it.

His ruminations were broken in upon by the arrival of Mr Walters. The little man was in high gig over the result of the sale.

'Above twenty-three thousand pounds it will be, Mr Tattersall tells me, after he has taken his toll of it. That allows ample for the paying off at Lambourne without encroaching on Sir Rollo's demands and leaves a little over for Mr Rodney — if I can arrange it without his father's knowledge.'

'Rodney is my concern now, Ned. Do not be putting yourself to the trouble of falsifying accounts, it won't fadge and you know it. Sir Rollo's no sapskull.'

Walters sighed in obvious relief. 'You've taken a weight off my mind and no mistake, my lord. What had you in view for the lad, if I may make so bold as to ask?'

'I'll try for a commission in my old regiment for him. If that doesn't answer, then I'll do the best I can. A glass of wine?"

'Thank you, my lord.' The agent hesitated before adding, 'Sir Rollo's not going to be best pleased at this. I've a notion he was set on the marriage.'

'Why, d'you know, Ned? I dare say it is all very fine to betroth one's son to an heiress but her father is still alive and it cannot be supposed that he would be willing to frank both Rodney and Sir Rollo — not, at all events, until the wedding takes place and that, I believe, will not be for a year at least.' It was plain from the anguished expression on Walter's face that he was wrestling with his conscience over the fine point of whether his devotion to Rodney should take precedence over his loyalty to his master. Penston laughed suddenly. 'Let me help you, Ned. What will happen at Lambourne if Rodney goes?'

'It will be sold up, never a doubt of it. Sir Rollo'll not come back there to live.'

'And you?'

'I'd go, too, my lord.'

Lord Penston toyed idly with a paperweight on his desk. 'Your father has grown old in the service of mine,' he said thoughtfully, 'but it would break his heart did I bring in a younger man over him. His son, perhaps, might be acceptable?'

'He'd as like heave a brick at my head, my lord!'

'You'd take the chance?'

'To go back to the Chase? I — I'd deem it an honour, my lord.' The little man's eyes glistened with unaccustomed moisture. 'I've only stayed on at Lambourne for Mr Rodney's sake. If he's not to be there, there's nothing to hold me.'

'Good!' said his lordship cheerfully. 'Then when this business is completed we will travel to the Chase together and talk to the Gaffer.' He laughed again at the look of apprehension on Ned Walter's face. 'Good God, man, you're full-grown and forty! He'll scarce beat you!'

The Gaffer's offspring shuddered at the very suggestion. 'Do you recall the day we took out the young gelding, my lord?'

'Aye, and ate our meals standing for a week! Damnation, Ned, that was all of twenty-five years ago! They were good days, though.'

'The best, my lord.' Walters seemed likely to lapse into a reminiscent vein but was checked sharply by his host's next question.

'What can you tell me of Mr Hammerton?'

'No more than you'd write on your thumbnail, my lord. If Sir Rollo has dealings with him then he does so from Brussels.'

'Dealings? What sort of dealings?'

'I couldn't say, my lord.'

'You could hazard a guess, Ned. All I am concerned with is to know how it will be to his advantage for his son to marry Hammerton's daughter. There can be no immediate profit else he would not have sold his stable — though I allow he can lose twenty thousand on the turn of a card. Come, let me have the truth.'

The little man drew out a spotted cotton handkerchief and mopped his forehead though the atmosphere in the big room was no more than pleasantly warm. 'You'll be the death of me, Mr

Guy,' he complained. 'I've no proof of what I say and I'd be glad if you forgot I ever said it, but it is my opinion that Mr Rodney is being pushed to this marriage as a sort of bribe.'

'A bribe? To Hammerton? Why should Sir Rollo do that?'

'Either to secure his business interests with the gentleman or, maybe, to keep his mouth shut.'

The fire crackled cosily in the ensuing silence and Penston leaned an arm on the mantelshelf to gaze into its depths.

'If your surmise is correct,' he said at last, 'what do you suppose will happen when the bribe is — er, removed?'

'That would depend on the urgency of the business. Mr Rodney will be twenty-one in a little over a year. After that, he is his own master.'

'Just so. Hence the necessity for contracting him to the young lady so that he cannot honourably cry off when he comes of age. There is no prior attachment, I take it?'

The agent smiled. 'Not on his part, my lord. I'd say he is not fully awake on that suit!'

Lord Penston raised a disbelieving eyebrow. 'What? Looking as he does and nigh on twenty? Don't gammon me, Ned! Speaking of suits, I wonder how he is prospering at this moment.'

'He might learn something, my lord, if he plays his cards aright.'

'He well might,' agreed Penston, kicking back a log that threatened to fall upon the hearth with a sublime disregard for his Hessians that would earn the reproach of his valet when he came to inspect them later. 'So let us contain ourselves until he returns and while the time away by discussing the alterations I wish to make at the Chase but dare not attempt because of incurring your father's displeasure!'

'I had suspected as much!' groaned Walters, in the manner of one philosophically accepting his unhappy lot, which attitude, he was pained to observe, merely aroused unfeeling amusement in the breast of his future employer.

CHAPTER
TWO

HAD anyone cared to enquire, which happily they did not, as to the subject matter of the book which so held Miss Patience Routledge's interest, she would have been obliged to confess that she had not the least idea of what it consisted.

Nor was it to be supposed that Miss Routledge was day-dreaming, for such a luxury was not to be indulged in by a paid companion, however well-bred and highly esteemed she might be. She was also a most agreeable-looking lady who, if not precisely in her first youth, yet possessed a delicacy of complexion and an elegance of form which many younger damsels might envy. The muslin mob-cap, edged with a lace frill and tied neatly under her chin, permitted a few soft curls of her dark brown hair to escape and frame a countenance remarkable for its sweetness of expression, although at that moment anxiety appeared to over-rule all other emotion. Every so often she allowed her eyes to rest upon the object of her concern who was seated only a few feet from her, her fingers busily netting a purse.

This young lady, tastefully attired in a spotted cambric round gown, with bodice *à l'enfant*, as befitted her scarcely attained sixteen years, gave every promise of developing into the Beauty that her father devoutly hoped would be the lot of his only child. Her short golden locks were arranged in most becoming curls over her small head and, although her figure was, as yet, slight and unformed, there was nothing of the child to be discerned in the cool level stare of her fine blue eyes nor in the firm moulding of her rounded chin and well-shaped mouth. No, thought Miss Routledge, one could not fault the girl's appearance but, though she was in general complaisant and her manners of the prettiest, the fact of her having spent all her life in the company of adults had robbed her of much natural exuberance and given her an air of mature self-possession which, to her companion's mind, might well prove to be an obstacle to the social success so desired for her by her parent.

Her intelligence was of the highest order and her mind well-informed far beyond that of most young ladies of her years, nor was it of the least use to tell her that gentlemen were not favourably impressed by ladies whose knowledge exceeded their own and who made no attempt to conceal that unfortunate fact. For, not to put too fine a point upon it, Miss Judith Hammerton displayed a distressing lack of inclination to conform to the male notion of what should be right and proper conduct in a chit not yet out of the schoolroom.

To cap it all, her father had declared that he had approved a husband for her and Miss Routledge had been warned to prepare the girl for her suitor's visit. Such heavy-handed dealing with his adored only child had moved her to astonished protest, but she had been curtly informed that his mind was quite made up and would she be so good as to carry out her duties. Thus adjured, Miss Routledge could only bow to the inevitable and pray that her charge did not take the young gentleman in strong dislike when he presented himself, which could happen as likely as not.

A soft chuckle interrupted her musings and she looked up quickly to find herself the object of Miss Hammerton's amused scrutiny.

'Dear Miss Patience,' she said in her clear young voice, 'do not be troubling yourself on my account, I beg of you. The gentleman is surely more to be pitied than I, who have a doting and considerate father, while his would appear to be a very odd sort of man, forever behindhand with the world, and with no notion of anything beyond his own pleasure nor any thought for his son, save only how best to get him off his hands.'

It said much for Miss Routledge's troubled frame of mind that she did not at once think to enquire as to the source of Miss Hammerton's information nor to reproach her for censuring in such terms a gentleman many years her senior.

'Indeed, I cannot truthfully find anything to commend in Sir Rollo's behaviour,' she confessed. 'To sell off his entire stables without regard for his son who has had the charge of them these two years past — oh, it is beyond anything! And the money—' She stopped abruptly, realizing where her thoughts were leading her, but Miss Hammerton chuckled again.

'Goes to Brussels, no doubt, to sustain Sir Rollo and his — ah, companion of the moment?'

'Judith! How dare you speak of such things!'

A small hand was laid on her arm. 'Because they exist. Pray recall, dear Miss Patience, you have been my mentor for only two months. Others have been less nice in their dealings with me or, perhaps, thought I would not understand their sly hints and quips.'

Miss Routledge bit her lip wondering, not for the first time, if, despite the nine-year difference in their ages, the girl's intellect and understanding were not greatly superior to her own. It was very true that, apart from her teachers, Judith had been left much to the mercy of servants and persons of inferior position. That she had grown up to be such a taking young lady, with no trace of cant or idiom in her speech, was greatly to her credit, but it could not be denied that her unusual situation had left its mark on her lively and impressionable mind.

'How did you learn of Sir Rollo's — affairs?'

The girl put aside her netting-box, and folded her hands composedly. 'In the usual way, through the servants. No, Miss Patience, I am not in the habit of discussing such things with them, but they fell into the way of talking before me in an unguarded manner, that is all.'

And quite enough! thought Miss Routledge grimly. Aloud she said: 'Lest you should wonder at *my* knowledge, I have a friend who resides near Lambourne in Essex and I took the liberty, when your father informed me of his plans, to write to her and ask what she knew of young Mr Nairn.'

'What did she say?'

The eagerness in the girl's voice betrayed her youth and Miss Routledge could not forbear to smile as she replied. 'He is well spoken of in the district, and is a most personable young man, sought after by all the ladies.'

'Oh!' said Miss Hammerton doubtfully.

'No!' said Miss Routledge. 'He has nothing of his father in

him but favours his mother who, although seven years dead, is still remembered with affection and respect.'

'But why should he want to wed me?' asked the girl in a wondering tone. 'Surely his case cannot be so desperate or he so bereft of family —'

'Judith, I do not know,' said Miss Routledge forthrightly. 'I can tell you the whole business has had me in a puzzle.' She paused and then plunged resolutely on. 'You are aware, I believe, that I was not always put to the necessity of earning my living?'

'But, of course. You are Lord Devereux's daughter, you have been presented at court and had your season in London. Had not your father ruined himself by one unlucky throw, you would now, doubtless, be mistress of a noble establishment with several hopeful children at your knee. When Lord Devereux died you devoted yourself to your stricken mother until she, too, departed this unhappy life.'

'Leaving her entire income to my dear and only brother in consideration of his providing a home for me,' supplemented Miss Routledge, apparently quite unmoved by this masterly summing-up of her previous existence.

'Which arrangement you could not care for, being a lady of independent spirit,' went on Miss Hammerton.

Miss Routledge nearly laughed. 'How well you know me, my dear!' she said ruefully. 'My brother had the best of it. My mother's money to supplement his own and another pair of hands — mine! — to assist in the house at no charge to himself, except for my food.'

'And his wife?'

'I have the highest opinion of my sister-in-law,' said Miss Routledge firmly, 'but to be forever dependent on her good nature was more than I could endure. Oh, I know my poor mother deplored my love of freedom and thought, by depriving me of any income, to rivet me to my brother's household —' She stopped suddenly. 'My dear Judith, pray forgive me. None of this is your concern and the telling of it cannot be of any interest to you. I cannot imagine why I embarked upon it.'

'It interests me very much,' said Miss Hammerton simply.

'What I wish to know is how you came to hear of this situation.'

'Ah, yes, that was a trifle strange, I grant you,' admitted Miss Routledge. 'It was through Lord Yeovil, a cousin of my mother's. We were all spending last Christmas under his roof when he drew me aside one evening and said that Richard — my brother — had told him of my wish to seek some genteel employment. While he much deplored my intention and failed to see the necessity for it, it had come to his notice that such a post as might admirably become my limited talents was on offer.'

'But how could he know of it? What has my father to do with Lord Yeovil?' asked Judith wonderingly.

'Nothing, I think. I do not believe that Yeovil even knew your father's name. But at one time he was a close friend of Sir Rollo Nairn's and Sir Rollo, knowing that *his* recommendation would hardly procure the respectable sort of female your father had in mind, appealed to Yeovil. I fitted the description to a nicety.'

' "A generous emolument is offered to a lady of breeding and fashionable accomplishments by a respectable widowed gentleman, wishful of preparing his daughter for entry into polite society." Oh, yes! I wrote it out for him. But I must ask you, Miss Patience, as you knew of Sir Rollo's interest in all this, did you not also know of his intent to wed me to his son?'

'No, 'pon honour! Though when your father told me, a month since, I was not over surprised. I collect they are close friends, your father and Sir Rollo?'

'Friends?' repeated Judith slowly. 'That I do not know. But there is some strong tie that binds them to each other, of that I am certain. The only time Sir Rollo came to this house was in the summer of last year. I was presented — to be looked over, I think. He seemed pleased enough with what he saw but it was far otherwise with me.'

'What was he like?' asked Miss Routledge curiously, knowing it to be improper of her to ask but unable to forbear from doing so.

'Not what you might imagine. A well-formed man of medium height, dark hair touched with silver, and a practised smile. Personable enough and of considerable address, but with no great claim to distinction. Perhaps I am not of the right generation to appreciate his charms, but all the while he was speaking to me his eyes were busy about my person in such fashion that, had my father not been present, I should have been strongly tempted to box his ears!"

'He was, of course, considering you as a possible bride for his son,' suggested Miss Routledge in what, even to herself, sounded an unconvincing tone.

'Then if his son looks upon me in like manner when he calls I'll have none of him, and that I promise you!" declared Miss Hammerton roundly.

Miss Routledge almost shuddered at the thought of the repercussions that could ensue as the result of her charge's defiance. She had not spoken with Mr Hammerton above half-a-score of times in the two months she had been at Bury Street, for he was rarely in residence at the house, but that was sufficient to breed in her a healthy respect for her employer. Liking for him she had none nor, to be fair, did he appear to expect any such emotion to be expended upon him, but regard, even affection, for his daughter he did look for in her companion and, once assured of its existence, seemed well content to sit back and leave the handling of affairs to Miss Routledge.

Should, however, matters take a turn other than he would wish, she had no doubt she would be called to account for the offence, and could readily imagine herself outside the street door with her valises beside her before the cat could lick its ear.

With this daunting prospect in mind, she began hesitantly to suggest to Miss Hammerton that the forthcoming interview with Mr Nairn be approached in a fairminded spirit.

'After all is said, he is in no better case than you, as you yourself acknowledge. Reserve your opinion, my dear, until — what is it? What are you looking at?'

Miss Hammerton had risen and was standing by the window, staring down into the street, her attention wholly captured by what she saw there.

'Unless I am quite mistaken,' she said slowly, 'Mr Nairn is, at this very moment, approaching the house.' Miss Routledge sprang to her feet and, hurrying to the window, was just in time to see the young gentleman who had been standing hesitantly on the opposite side of the road, apparently come to a decision for, setting his high-crowned beaver more firmly on his head, he squared his shoulders and stepped forward with the air of one about to take part in a cavalry charge, the outcome of which might very well prove fatal. As he disappeared from her view Miss Hammerton emitted a long sigh. 'He is prodigiously handsome,' she breathed, 'and with a pronounced air of fashion, I do declare!'

The imperative ringing of the street bell urged Miss Routledge to a sense of her duties and she cast a critical eye over her charge's appearance.

'That gown will never do, my dear,' she decreed. 'The yellow crape that came from the dressmaker yesterday would be more the thing. One cannot be too careful in the first trenches of an acquaintance to leave just the right impression.'

Swiftly she hustled the young lady to her room, foiling any attempt on her part to peep through the balusters for a glimpse of her suitor as Jessop, Mr Hammerton's pontifical butler, conducted him across the hall.

'If you will step this way, sir, I will inform Mr Hammerton of your arrival.'

Rodney, feeling not a little apprehensive, allowed himself to be ushered into a small, but handsomely appointed room. A quick inspection of his surroundings convinced him that the elegant furnishings, the rich brocade drapes and the fine Waterford glass chandelier, its chains swathed in sleeves of silk, were hardly to be looked for in a house rented out for the season, so it was to be supposed that Mr Hammerton intended a lengthy stay in Bury Street if he had gone to the expense of conveying his own furnishings thither. The room displayed marked evidence of the feminine taste in a most superior chaise-longue, a draped work-table, and a lady's secretary fashioned out of black rosewood, with tulip cross-banding, and elaborately ornamented with brass. Rodney, whose taste for fine furniture was instinctive rather than instructed, was inspecting this latter piece with lively interest when the door opened behind him and he spun round on his heel to meet the amused regard of one of the largest gentlemen he had ever beheld in all his life.

Though close on six feet himself, Mr Hammerton towered over him by some five or six inches and his whole person was in proportion. He had clearly just returned from riding for he was still attired in buckskins and boots, while his coat was flung open to display an expanse of scarlet waistcoat, embellished with gilt buttons. His countenance, though not precisely handsome, was pleasing enough, the entire expression being dominated by deep-set, heavy-lidded eyes that appeared to miss nothing of what went on around him. Rodney, considerably taken aback at sight of this formidable-looking personage, sufficiently remembered his manners to utter the customary platitudes.

'Your servant, sir. I — I am Rodney Nairn. I believe my father informed you that I should have to be in London at this time and would give myself the pleasure of making your acquaintance.' He paused uncertainly, wondering if he should say more of his father's intentions.

'Aye, he did that.' The deep voice held the faintest hint of a Yorkshire burr. 'No very pleasant thing for you, I dare say, this sale.'

'No, sir,' admitted Rodney.

'Well, that's your father's way and who should know it better than you? And now he's pressing you into marrying my girl. Is that any more to your taste?'

To Rodney's over-anxious ear there was a note of faint contempt underlying this utterance which worked so powerfully on his sensibilities that he could not but express what was in his mind.

'No, sir, it is not!' he burst out, then, realizing that such a declaration was hardly polite, either to his host or to his host's daughter, he hastily proffered an apology for his ill-bred vehemence. Mr Hammerton listened to him in silence, a faint smile touching his hard mouth. Then, hands on hips, he walked slowly around the young man, inspecting his person and apparel in the most minute and particular detail.

Rodney, scarlet with embarrassment and anger, hardly knew how to contain himself during this humiliating scrutiny and tried to pass it off with a jest.

'Light-fleshed, you'll be bound to say, sir, but time will

remedy that, and there's sound breeding on both sides!'

Mr Hammerton appeared to take this remark quite seriously. 'You've a fine pair of shoulders and I dare say you will fill out to match 'em. Good legs, too. Yes, I will allow you to be a pretty boy enough. No doubt you would sire me handsome grandchildren.'

Rodney's hands clenched involuntarily at his sides and his eyes flashed fire as he rapped out: 'Damme, sir, I'm no stallion to be bought for stud!'

Mr Hammerton flung back his head and shouted with laughter. 'Make no mistake, my young buck, that's just what you are!' he retorted. 'But I like your spirit, though you are far from being up to everything. Age and the good Lord will attend to that, but you are not ripe for marriage yet, nor is my Judith.'

'Sir,' said Mr Nairn, all icy courtesy. 'I deplore the necessity for having to inform you that such is not my intention. Believe me, I mean no disrespect to you or your daughter, but I — I have no mind for matrimony.'

The laughter faded from Mr Hammerton's eyes, leaving them cold and watchful. In the ensuing silence, Rodney found his glance dwelling upon the riding whip which the big man had tossed carelessly on to a table as he had entered the room and it crossed his mind to wonder if he would be offered physical violence. But Mr Hammerton's manner was civil enough when he spoke.

· 'And what, then, is your intention, if I may make so bold as to enquire?'

Rodney swallowed and stood silent for a moment. While on the one hand he was persuaded he owed this man some explanation for his conduct, on the other, his godfather had straitly charged him on no account to divulge his plans to one who must be bound to oppose them. He endeavoured to temporize with small success.

'I — as you so rightly observe, sir, I am not ripe for marriage. To get out into the world I believe to be an object worthy of the highest consideration, and a few years' more experience should render me a vastly more eligible husband for — for any lady.'

'Where had you thought to glean your experience, Mr Nairn?

Quietly though the words were spoken, Rodney felt much like a very small mouse confronted by a very large cat. Mr Hammerton laughed again, but softly. 'Come, young sir, let us be plain with each other. Thanks to your care of them, your father's horses fetched a good price to-day — no, I was not at the Corner, but there were those who kept me informed. The dibs are in tune for Sir Rollo now and he will be on the best of terms with himself, but you know as well as I that in a month's time he could be all to pieces again with his pockets to let. So,' went on this surprising gentleman coolly, 'if you want to make your break with him, now is the time to do it. What had you in mind?'

'To join the army in the Peninsula!'

Rodney could not afterwards be sure quite how it was he came to confess his intention but, strangely, his prospective father-in-law appeared to sympathize with his ambition for he nodded his head several times slowly before replying.

'A hard school and a telling one. But how shall you contrive? Oh, I've a very fair notion of how you are placed — little money and no prospects.'

'My godfather, Lord Penston, is attending to everything for me,' said Rodney, very much on his dignity but wondering how he was going to explain his extraordinary lapse to his godfather.

'I had not known of this connection!' Mr Hammerton's tone was sharp with surprise.

'It is hardly to be wondered at. I had not seen Lord Penston myself these six years and more until this morning at Tattersall's. Do you know him, sir?'

'Let us say I know of him. No doubt he will be trying for a commission in his old regiment for you?'

'Yes, but if that cannot be arranged speedily then I must take whatever offers.'

'Then you must,' agreed Mr Hammerton. 'Speed is of the essence for none of this will please your father.' Then, seeing the anxious question in Rodney's eyes, he stepped forward and clapped his big hands on the young man's shoulders. 'Your secret is safe with me, lad. I like your mettle and I think you have got a lot of good sense in the cockloft of yours. If, in a few years' time, you should feel inclined to call upon me again — of your own free will, mind! — then I shall be pleased to see you.'

There was no mistaking the tenor of this speech and Rodney, to his intense mortification, found himself colouring up warmly. 'Depend upon it, sir, you will have no need of me in a few years' time,' he protested. 'Your daughter —'

'Will marry no one without my consent and that gives you close on five years until she is twenty-one. I'll not mince matters. My blunt could buy a title for my girl to-morrow but I would like to see her wed to something better than a brothel bully or some adipose Adonis of the Prince Regent's set.' As he spoke he walked over to a bell-pull and tugged it sharply. 'There's someone I would like to make your acquaintance, Miss Routledge, who acts as my daughter's companion, chaperone — call her what you will. My own dear wife being dead these many years, it was necessary that I should commission a lady of unimpeachable standing to instruct Judith in how she should go on. She has been used to living quiet in the country and not seeing many folk, apart from a few neighbours. I thought a visit to London under the guidance of Miss Routledge would make it easier for her to withstand the impact of the haut ton when she makes her come-out.'

'And that will be next year, sir?'

'Or the one following. She is but a schoolroom miss yet and I've no wish to see her forced up like a hothouse plant before she is ready for it. Jessop,' he said to the butler who had answered his ring, 'ask Miss Routledge to be good enough to step down here for a moment, would you? Now, Mr Nairn, what can I offer you — Madeira, sherry, or do your nerves stand in need of a clap of thunder?'

The friendly grin which accompanied these last words did more good for Rodney's nerves than the proffered brandy could have done and, smiling shyly, he accepted a glass of excellent sherry and was chatting in the most natural and amicable manner with his host when Jessop swept open the door to announce:

'Miss Routledge, sir.'

Mr Hammerton then presented him to a tall, pleasant-looking lady, dressed with simple good taste in a gown of Indian muslin, trimmed with blonde lace, whose air of well-bred consequence set him further at his ease. In no time at all he found himself responding to her friendly interest and, gently prompted by Mr Hammerton, got to telling her all about The Centaur and his godfather, and how the latter had rescued the former. Miss Routledge nodded her approval of Lord Penston's action.

'I am persuaded he did just as he ought,' she declared warmly. 'Your father cannot have intended your horse to be sold with the rest.'

Mr Nairn, not being in full agreement with her on that point, thought it best to change the subject. 'Do you intend a lengthy stay in London, sir?' he enquired of Mr Hammerton.

The large gentleman shrugged slightly and looked at the lady. 'That is for Miss Routledge to say.'

'I cannot imagine why we should,' she returned candidly. 'For Judith — Miss Hammerton, is not yet out and, apart from indulging our fancies for modish apparel and seeing the sights, there is nothing to be gained by remaining here throughout the whole season. I must warn you, sir,' she added, addressing herself to her employer, 'that we viewed Miss Mary Linwood's Gallery of Pictures in Worsted this morning and Judith was so taken by the almost magical effect of this art that she believes it only proper to attempt a portrait of you after the same style!'

'If she expects me to sit unmoving by the hour while she practices her stitchery,' said Miss Hammerton's unappreciative parent, 'that, let me tell you, is coming it a bit too strong!'

The conversation proceeded on these pleasant, if uninstructive, lines for a few more minutes. Rodney gathered that Mr Hammerton's country residence was near Odiham in Hampshire but, apart from this intelligence, he could glean nothing more of his host's circumstances nor any clue as to his connection with Sir Rollo. Nor, did it appear, was he to be granted the pleasure of meeting Miss Hammerton. He caught an enquiring glance directed at Mr Hammerton by Miss Routledge but could discern no perceptible response on that gentleman's impassive countenance.

After half-an-hour had passed, Rodney judged it prudent to bring his visit to a close, and both lady and gentleman accompanied him to the hall where Jessop was waiting to hand him his hat and gloves. As he turned to take his leave of Miss Routledge, a slight movement on the landing above caught his attention and he looked up to behold a young lady standing there, her gaze earnestly directed upon him. An open door behind her permitted the spring sunshine to stream through, transforming her into a very figure of gold or, as it seemed to Rodney's dazzled eyes, a yellow-robed angel with a nimbus of light about her fair head. Seeing his stupefaction, Miss Routledge looked up also and, at once, the vision disappeared and the closing of the door shut out the sunlight.

Rodney completed his adieux and took his leave in a reasonably composed manner but, once outside, he crossed the street and turned to look up at the house. She stood at a second-floor window, watching him, no longer an angel of light but a lovely, golden-haired girl in a yellow dress. For a moment they gazed upon each other then, as if by mutual agreement, each began to smile; his hand went up to remove his hat; hers was raised in a shy gesture of farewell. Then she moved away and was gone, leaving him still staring upwards, hat in hand, until brought to his senses by the entreaties of a porter who was attempting to convey a heavy trunk from a delivery wagon to the house in front of which he was standing.

'Move up there, young sir, *hif* you please! There's some of us 'as work to do!'

'Oh? Yes, of course!' Rodney hastily replaced his hat and walked on, leaving the delivery man staring after him.

'Fair beetleheaded, 'e be!' the porter remarked to the world in general as he let his trunk down urgently on the doorstep. 'Git away, you!' he added, aiming a kick at a stray mongrel that had ventured near to sniff. 'What was 'e a-gawpin' at, anyway?'

But when he turned to scrutinize No. 26, no vision of loveliness presented itself to his hopeful gaze and he was recalled to his duties by the strident tones of a far from lovely maidservant who stood, hands on hips, scowling at him over the top of the trunk, and demanding to know if he would oblige her by removing so bulky an article from off her newly-scoured doorstep so that decent folk could step in and out of the house.

*   *   *

Miss Hammerton's fleeting appearance on the landing had also been observed by her father, nor had Mr Nairn's response to it escaped his notice, and there was a marked twinkle in his eye when he invited Miss Routledge to rejoin him in the drawing-room.

'That was a most telling pose of Judith's,' he chuckled. 'Had you arranged it?'

'Certainly not!' she retorted. 'But I confess I was at a loss to know why you did not summon her to meet Mr Nairn.'

'Because,' he said coolly, 'I saw no object in presenting a gentleman who has declared himself unwilling to pay his addresses to her.'

'Unwilling?' gasped Miss Routledge. 'But I thought it to be an arranged thing, that —'

'It would seem that Mr Nairn has a mind of his own,' interrupted Mr Hammerton curtly. 'What did you make of him?'

'I thought him particularly gentlemanlike and quite above the ordinary for good looks. What an excessively handsome couple they would make, he and Judith.'

'They well may in time, so I was not taking the risk of her frightening him off with her quick tongue!' explained Judith's father. 'He's scarce out of leading strings yet, a few years in the army and he will be less of a Johnny Raw.'

'A few years in the army and he could well be dead!' pointed out Miss Routledge sensibly. 'What am I to say to Judith?'

'I'll talk to her,' said Mr Hammerton. 'But, first, I have something to say to you, ma'am. I would like to have your assurance that, should any — misfortune befall me, you will continue to reside with Judith and watch over her, at least until she comes of age. In such circumstances your present emolument will be trebled and you will become a trustee of my daughter's estate, together with John Faber, my attorney. You know my wishes for her future, that she should take her place in the world that is hers by right, or perhaps I should say by right of her mother's birth, and that she should form an eligible connection and marry securely into that world. This,' he went on in an oddly hesitant voice, much at variance with his normally composed manner, 'I promised her mother I would do. It was her last request of me.'

'Then why,' asked Miss Routledge, moved in spite of herself by Mr Hammerton's unwonted display of sensitivity, 'did you not secure Mr Nairn for her?'

'It would not answer if the lad is not willing. I'll not have his father force him to it.'

Miss Routledge thought it prudent to ask no more questions. 'I will endeavour to be worthy of your trust, sir,' she said quietly. 'Though I pray my guardianship may never be called for and that you will, very soon, be proudly handing Judith over to some worthy gentleman. I will summon her to you.'

With that she left him and returned to the schoolroom to find Miss Hammerton standing in the centre of it with such a woebegone expression on her usually serene countenance that Miss Routledge cried out.

'My dear child — no! You must not take it to heart so!'

'My father has sent him away, has he not?'

'He — Mr Nairn — is not wishful of setting up his establishment until he has seen more of the world and your father is in agreement with him. Come, Judith!' Miss Routledge essayed a laugh in an effort to elevate the girl's spirits. 'He is but your first suitor! There will be many more.'

'But not like him.' Miss Hammerton spoke with a strange finality. 'Nor can I suppose him to be entirely indifferent to me.'

'How should you know that?' asked her startled perceptress.

'He turned to look for me when he left the house, and smiled up at me,' murmured Miss Hammerton dreamily.

'Judith! You were never peeping from the window?' cried the horrified Miss Routledge. 'Such conduct in a young lady is — well, it is not at all the thing!'

She might have saved her breath for all the notice her charge took of her strictures.

'Is he coming back, do you know?'

Miss Routledge had to confess that he was not. 'He is entering the army, I understand. But your father can give you all the ins and outs of it better than I. Will you go down to him, my dear?'

'Yes, yes, of course.' Miss Hammerton paused by the door for a moment, her hand resting on the ornate brass knob. 'Miss Patience, is it immodest in me to confess that I liked him very well?'

Miss Routledge smiled indulgently. 'Foolish child! You did not even speak to him!'

'No, and it was a great deal too bad of my father not to have presented him to me and so I shall tell him!' declared Miss Hammerton with spirit. 'Another thing I shall tell him, that however many suitors he may parade for my inspection, they all must measure up in some fashion to Mr Nairn!'

So saying, she departed, leaving an amused Miss Routledge to reflect on the startling effect a personable young man could have upon even the most level-headed of damsels. Mr. Nairn, she was prepared to wager, would be forgotten in the first weeks of a London season, if not long before. Then she fell to thinking over the rather strange conversation she had just had with her employer and whether she had been altogether prudent in taking on the responsibility of Judith should any ill chance befall her father. And why should Mr Hammerton be apprehensive of the future?

Further cogitation was denied her by the entry of the housekeeper, who expressed a wish to confer with her on the scarcity of bed-linen, of which not a great supply had been brought to Bury Street from Odiham, no one being very clear as to the probable length of their stay in London, so together they went upstairs to view the shortcomings of the linen closet.

CHAPTER THREE

'IT is very tiresome, to be sure, that we should be obliged to wait upon his lordship's convenience, but on this occasion, I am persuaded it is the only course open to us,' pronounced the Dowager Lady Quendon, settling herself more comfortably in her massive wing-chair, drawn close to the fireplace from which, every so often, there rose a small puff of smoke to drift through the room.

The saloon at Netherdene was pretentious rather than handsome, its furnishings heavy and tasteless. Indeed, the whole gave an impression of disuse which was hardly to be wondered at since the late Viscount had proclaimed it to be a damned draughty room and not worth the expense of heating. His lady, being of a parsimonious nature, promptly closed it and shrouded the furniture in Holland covers, which were removed only for some outstanding occasion of family or national significance.

On this particular end-of-April afternoon, there were present, besides the dowager, her daughter Euphrasia, and her late husband's cousin, Mr Jasper Edgecombe. The young lady, seated opposite her mother, was working diligently upon her tapestry, though any close observer might be pardoned for wondering whether the ill-set stitches were occasioned by the indifferent light or by the nervous apprehension apparent in Miss Edgecombe's bearing.

She was a pallid, slender girl of twenty, with few pretensions to beauty and an air of uncertainty which did nothing to mitigate this unfortunate circumstance. Her large brown eyes protruded under heavy dark brows; her teeth, though white and regular enough, also thrust themselves forward, giving her mouth a pouting appearance, while her nose was straight and well formed, yet had a pinched air about the nostrils that seemed to indicate that its owner considered herself to be on a plane above many other less fortunate beings.

The dowager was at pains to shelter her only child from the harsher truths of life on the grounds of her supposedly delicate health, and on this occasion, being quite determined that Euphrasia should show to the best advantage, she surveyed with satisfaction her daughter's vastly unbecoming gown of straw-coloured sarsenet, worn with a brown velvet spencer and ornamented at the neckline by a deep lace frill. Most of this handsome get-out was concealed under an Indian shawl, which was pinned across Miss Edgecombe's bosom to protect her from the piercing draughts that pervaded the room.

'I must own, my dear,' stated the dowager in the tone of one accustomed to having her opinions deferred to, 'that I am not altogether happy with the style of hair arrangement you favour.'

'But, mama, it is all the go — à la Titus, you know. Is it not so, cousin Jasper?'

Mr Jasper Edgecombe, when directly appealed to had, perforce, to support his cousin. 'Oh, indeed, I assure you, ma'am, a very knowing cut and bang up to the mark. Vastly becoming, too,' he added, bestowing on Euphrasia the cursory regard of one who has known the damsel all her life and fails to see anything commendable in her appearance.

She cast him a grateful glance and wished with all her heart that the present unhappy circumstances did not render him ineligible as a suitor, for Mr Edgecombe, entering upon his thirtieth year, was a very pretty figure of a man. His coat of dark-blue superfine set off his powerful shoulders to a nicety, while his striped marcella waistcoat had several of its gilt buttons left undone the better to display his high starched shirt points and a neckcloth fashioned in a very creditable Mathematical style. Mulberry-hued trousers and half-boots completed an appearance which, if not precisely dandified, yet conveyed a distinct air of fashion. His countenance was animated in expression, being dominated by a strong aquiline nose and a pair of very alert blue eyes; his brown hair was becomingly disarranged, and his ready smile and easy manners lent support to the general opinion that he was a pleasant, gentlemanlike sort of man.

Lady Quendon, however, had other and more pressing matters to occupy her attention than Mr Edgecombe's prepossessing appearance.

'I can only hope,' she said in a far from sanguine tone, 'that Captain Sir Rodney Nairn — I beg his pardon, Lord Quendon, is not one of your fashionable town beaux who does not sit down to his dinner before seven or eight o'clock. That will never do for Netherdene and so I shall inform him.'

'But what if he asks us to remove to the Dower House, mama?' Euphrasia's remark was, perhaps, more notable for commonsense than tact, but the dowager was not a whit put out by it.

'I cannot imagine that he will,' she declared, 'being in a somewhat equivocal position as well you know. For Sir Rollo to have disappeared in so — so thoughtless a way after the Duchess of Richmond's ball last year has placed his son in a sad quandary, and I cannot wonder at it that he has been loath to present himself here to claim the title.'

Mr Edgecombe pursed his lips and looked doubtful. 'That can hardly signify,' he observed. 'The worst that can be said of him is that he is outrunning the carpenter. His affairs cannot be at a stand forever because his father's demise cannot be proved. I understand he has spent much time in Brussels since he sold out of the army, endeavouring to trace Sir Rollo's movements on that fatal evening but, with the engagement at Waterloo coming so hard upon it and the general confusion that prevailed at that time, it is small wonder he has met with no success.'

This reasoned expression of opinion did not meet with the dowager's approval. 'While I have every respect for the goodness of heart that causes you to take such a tolerant view, Jasper,' she admonished him, 'I cannot feel it to be all the thing for a young gentleman to assume his father's dignities until he is assured that he has a right to do so.'

'But, mama, nothing may ever be proven! Would you have him wait all his life for titles that will be his in any event?'

'Some limit, I allow, must be set,' agreed her ladyship. 'But all this is profitless conjecture and a great waste of time. Even if Sir

Rollo is no more, that cannot help your case, Jasper.'

'Dear Lady Quendon,' said Mr Edgecombe smoothly, 'I have never deluded myself into thinking that I would step into his late lordship's shoes. That, you must agree, would be straining the caprices of Dame Fortune rather far.'

The dowager permitted herself a sniff. 'I have always understood the Peninsular service to be a dangerous one,' she responded. 'It certainly accounted for the life of my younger stepson, and Captain Nairn, I am given to understand, went on to take part in many hazardous engagements in France. It could not have been thought surprising had he failed to survive.'

'"A consummation devoutly to be wished!"' murmured Mr Edgecombe. 'Fie upon you, ma'am, for harbouring so uncharitable a sentiment!'

'My dear Jasper,' countered her ladyship pleasantly enough, because she had no wish to quarrel with Mr Edgecombe who, even if ineligible as a son-in-law, might still have his uses, 'when I feel called upon to seek your approbation upon the nature of my sentiments, then so I will inform you. Great Heaven, how dark it has become! Pray summon Brough, Euphrasia, and require him to bring more candles.'

At that moment her butler presented himself to her notice to announce that a chaise had been sighted proceeding up the drive at a smart pace. A few minutes later the sound of movement in the outer hall and yet another draught added to those already rampaging about the saloon informed the waiting company that their vigil was at an end.

Euphrasia hastily tidied away her woolwork while the dowager, requesting Mr Edgecombe to adjust the pole-screen that protected her from the fire, gave no sign whatever of having heard an arrival and continued to indulge herself in a lengthy monologue upon the eccentricities of Fate. Thus it was that Miss Edgecombe was best placed to observe the entrance of the newcomer. One glance at her slightly opened mouth and air of startled appreciation prompted her cousin to turn quickly towards the door. The elegant picture that greeted his perceptive stare caused him to entertain certain misgivings concerning the niceties of his own dress and to wonder whether he had not, perhaps, been rusticating for rather too long away from London.

Five years in the service of his country had wrought a considerable change in Rodney Nairn. His graceful figure, broadened to manly proportions, was displayed to advantage in superbly tailored coat and immaculate pantaloons. Above his plain buff waistcoat rose crisp shirt points, at least two inches taller than those affected by Mr Edgecombe, while the fall of his neckcloth in an impeccable Trône d'Amour was the work of an artist. Small gold tassels swung from his gleaming Hessians as he advanced into the room, his heavy-lashed grey eyes observing with lively interest the three persons there awaiting him.

As none of these made any effort to greet him he addressed himself to the impressive lady, gowned in magenta satin with matching turban set straight upon her greying locks, who was regarding him fixedly out of frosty blue eyes.

'Lady Quendon? Pray forgive me if I have kept you waiting, but I was detained in leaving London else I would have been with you an hour since.'

'Think nothing of it, my lord,' she responded, extending him her hand in a regal gesture. 'As I remember, no precise hour was set for your arrival.'

Lightly kissing the tips of her fingers, Rodney flashed her a sparkling glance. 'Another instance of my laxity,' he sighed. 'I fear my campaigning days have rendered me so far abroad in genteel usage, dear lady, that you will have to take me in hand, I dare say, and teach me how I should go on.'

This audacious little speech was accompanied by so sweet a smile that Lady Quendon found herself quite in harmony with the young man whose very existence she had so resented a few moments before, and she lost no time in presenting him to her daughter. Euphrasia, between shyness and excitement at meeting so interesting a gentleman, managed to look quite attractive and Rodney, who at first sight had put her down as a poor little dab of a girl, wanting in presence and countenance, felt he had done her less than justice.

'Mark my words,' Lord Penston had warned him, 'the old lady will do her possible to snare you for a son-in-law. That way she may stay on at Netherdene in all her former state.'

Rodney, who had no wish to dispossess the lady, nor any intention of being trapped into matrimony, had been amused at the suggestion. 'But you say there is a very presentable distant cousin?'

'Yes, your heir. He would have done very nicely for Miss Edgecombe had you not returned safe after Waterloo. I am not conversant with his claim to succession, but Lady Quendon appears well satisfied.'

As Mr Jasper Edgecombe stepped forward to greet him with outstretched hand and ready smile, the new Viscount suffered a sharp stab of surprise, almost of recognition. This, he reminded himself, was the man he had disappointed of his inheritance, and was expected to supplant in the lady's affections, yet there was something so compellingly familiar about his person and demeanour that to hail him as bosom friend would hardly seem inappropriate. Courteously he responded to Mr Edgecombe's gracefully turned phrases of welcome, wondering that he should be put in mind of nothing so much as some beast of prey seeking to lull its victim's suspicions before springing upon it and rending it to pieces. But Mr Edgecombe gave no sign of doing any such thing. On the contrary he was all affability, smoothing over any possible awkwardness in the occasion by his animated conversation and drawing Rodney on to speak of his military career, of fashionable London, of gay Brussels, and even of the search for his father.

'There, I fear, I am at Point-Non-Plus,' the Viscount had to admit. 'The Duke himself offered me every assistance in pursuing my enquiries, but all to no avail. My father just walked out of that ballroom and was never seen again. I called on his —' he hesitated and went on quickly, 'his closest friends, but none could tell me anything to the point so I must presume his disappearance was no pre-arranged thing, he had not planned to leave Brussels or anything of that sort.'

'Then it was either an unhappy accident or —' Mr Edgecombe raised an enquiring eyebrow.

'Just so. And if an accident, surely I would have had news of it, though I allow there were many such in the confusion that prevailed at that time.'

'He had enemies?'

Rodney smiled wryly. 'I have small doubt of it. His was not a conciliatory nature.'

Mr Edgecombe appeared prepared to discuss the matter further but Lady Quendon had heard enough on the subject.

'This is all very distressing, to be sure,' she declared, 'and especially for you, his son, to be forced to pursue such enquiries. But I am truly of the belief that the body is the better for the refreshment the mind receives in doing its duty, and nothing but good can result from your diligent endeavours.'

This lofty proclamation quite took away her audience's breath and the ensuing silence was broken by Brough, entering to enquire at what hour her ladyship desired dinner to be served.

'Why, at five o'clock, I should suppose.' Then, as the butler coughed gently and glanced at the long-case clock standing in the corner of the saloon, she frowned and continued rather crossly. 'I had not the least idea of the time. No doubt, Quendon, you will be wishful of changing your clothes after your journey?'

'Indeed I am in no case to sit down to table with you, ma'am,' began Rodney, when Mr Edgecombe swiftly intervened.

'Nor, to be truthful, am I,' he declared, 'but if her ladyship will overlook such informal attire, then perhaps the day and the dinner may be saved.'

'In general, I do not approve of gentlemen sitting down to dine in their walking or travelling dress,' stated the dowager. 'But I am of the opinion that, on this occasion, such laxness must be acceptable. Brough, show his lordship to his room. We will dine in half an hour.'

The dinner set before them, to Rodney's way of thinking, scarcely merited the consideration given it, being more of a substantial than an appetizing nature. Her ladyship, however, seemed well pleased with it and pontificated upon her sure knowledge of the culinary tastes of young gentlemen.

'Though, unhappily, not blessed with a son of my own and now bereft of my two stepsons, I am not quite without experience in these matters. I encouraged my late dear husband to partake of plain, good food and that, be assured, was always set

before him. Euphrasia, my dear, pray do attempt a morsel of this
fricassée of rabbit. I had cook prepare it especially for you. Such
a delicate appetite as she has,' she confided to Rodney, 'I vow
I am at my wits' end at times how best to tempt her.'

However the late Viscount's taste in food may have been
directed by his wife, it was a source of intense gratification to his
successor to discover that in the matter of choosing his wines he
had followed his own inclinations to happy effect. When Lady
Quendon had borne Euphrasia off with an arch reminder to the
gentlemen not to linger too long as she was having the whist table
set up in the drawing-room, Rodney, with a mental sigh of relief,
stretched out his legs in front of the fire and motioned to Mr
Edgecombe to pull up his chair and join him.

'Do they always dine in this mausoleum?' he enquired,
looking about the vast panelled room, its flickering wall-sconces
barely illuminating the dark corners.

'Oh, no, when alone or with one or two intimate guests, they
use the breakfast parlour. This dining-room is reserved for
Occasions.'

'I see,' murmured Rodney, helping himself to brandy and
sliding the bottle along the table to Mr Edgecombe. 'And am I,
then, an Occasion?'

'Unquestionably, my lord!' The hint of a smile touched Mr
Edgecombe's lips as he rose and, flipping up his coat-tails, stood,
glass in hand, with his back to the fire.

'So that is why we have to suffer the rigours of this ice-house.
My apologies, Edgecombe!'

'I assure you, Quendon, you have cause to be grateful to me
for arranging it so that we retained the warmth of our kerseymere
inexpressibles!' said Mr Edgecombe cheerfully. 'It is a fearsome
experience to be forced to don satin knee breeches at Netherdene
in the cooler months. I promise you that, upon one occasion,
standing as I am before this very fire, an awful smell of scorching
permeated the entire room. Satin, it would appear, is not so
resistant to direct heat as wool, and the flesh beneath was so
insensitive from the cold that disaster was only averted by my
hasty departure to the privacy of my bedchamber where I
stripped off the charred remains!'

'I trust you suffered no lasting hurt?' commiserated Rodney gravely.

'A trifle singed, but nothing to signify. What really put me out of humour was that, upon my return, his late lordship could not keep his tongue off the incident, remarking for ever on how he had often heard of hot *heads* but never of — you will know how it goes!'

'What manner of man was he?' asked Rodney curiously.

Mr Edgecombe drank deep of his brandy before replying. 'A clutch-fist,' he said at last. 'He and her ladyship were like two coats cut from the same cloth. A bruising rider with no more thought for his horse than his neck — which puts me in mind of what I would tell you. You will be wanting to ride about your estate to see what's what, so I presumed to bring over two of my cattle. There is nothing in the stables here other than the carriage horses and Euphrasia's hack, a spiritless beast and not up to your weight. I have got a lively young 'un that you might care to try, if not, there's my old Trumpeter that will carry you safe. You ride about twelve stone, I should guess?'

Rodney admitted that to be so and thanked Mr Edgecombe for his civility. 'I take it, then, that you do not live at Netherdene?'

'God forbid!' said Mr Edgecombe devoutly. 'Though I have run tame here since a lad. I manage a tight little estate situated some twenty miles from here. My aunt, whose property it is, keeps house for us and we go on very well together.'

'Twenty miles, eh?' mused the Viscount.

'Yes, just too far to be for ever dropping by, but convenient enough when urgently summoned!' The twist to his mouth as he uttered these words left Rodney in no doubt that Mr Edgecombe was frequently so summoned and harboured a high degree of resentment at such treatment.

'Forgive me, but I am not at all clear in my head as to the precise nature of our relationship,' he said, and was startled by the satirical expression that flashed over his companion's face, putting him so strongly in mind of some other that again he was tempted to believe he had encountered Mr Edgecombe in the past.

'Our connection is largely through the distaff side. My mother married her many times removed cousin, hence the reversion to the name of Edgecombe.' He nodded towards the brandy bottle. 'May I?'

'But of course. It is a remarkably fine spirit.'

Mr Edgecombe winked and laid a knowing finger to the side of his nose. 'Never paid duty, I'll be bound! The old lord did not believe in such nonsense — one of his few endearing traits.'

'You had no love for him, I take it?'

The other's eyes gleamed cold as steel. 'He treated me like a lackey and, when he died, left me not one penny piece.'

The frankness of the reply provoked Rodney into speaking his mind. 'To my way of thinking it would have been no wonderful thing if you had taken me in like aversion,' he said, and wondered at it when Mr Edgecombe flung back his head and laughed.

'On what count? You are Lord Quendon, none can dispute it.'

'There I would differ from you. That my father put a period to his life, or some other did so for him, is still not certain.'

'What of it? If he still lives, you are but holding his estates and dignities in trust for him.'

'Is that the generally held opinion?'

'By those with any commonsense, yes.' Mr Edgecombe tossed off his brandy and set down his glass. 'Think nothing of it, Quendon. I declare your conscience is too delicate!' Then, as if he had said rather more than he had intended, he continued in a different vein. 'There is one thing I had best warn you of, though I have no doubt her ladyship will inform you in detail later — indeed, I cannot conceive why she has not spoken of it before, unless it was that she feared you would take instant flight at the prospect! To-morrow is to be an Open Day at Netherdene. It is customarily held later in the year but, on learning of your imminent arrival, Lady Quendon decided it would be the very thing if you were present to delight the eyes of your visitors.'

'D'you mean I shall be expected to greet them?' asked the dismayed Viscount.

'Oh, yes,' asserted Mr Edgecombe. 'For you must understand you are something of a curiosity in the neighbourhood.'

'Doubtless like a performing bear, or a man with two heads!'

growled Rodney, not best pleased at this unexpected turn of events.

'Well, perhaps not precisely that,' allowed Mr Edgecombe. 'But you must agree that a certain amount of romantical mystery surrounds you. The gallant young seigneur bereft of his parent in so dramatic a fashion, comes to claim his own — as Gothic a situation as ever was!'

Rodney looked amused. 'You use the word "seigneur" — advisedly, perhaps? Do I also enjoy my "droit"?'

'That,' replied Mr Edgecombe with unction, 'I leave to your lordship to discover! Now, if you please, we had better remove to the drawing-room, else her ladyship will grow fretful.'

The dowager greeted their appearance with enthusiasm, and several rubbers of whist were entered upon, she losing no opportunity of criticizing her companions' play or of extolling her own superiority at the game. Having assured herself that Mr Edgecombe had broached the subject of the Open Day with Rodney, she made light of the matter, giving it as her opinion that the Viscount would do well to depress the pretensions of any visitor who thought to secure for himself more than the merest nod or bow in passing.

'Many worthy persons will attend, no doubt, and these Jasper or I will present to you as we see fit but do not, I beg of you, my dear Quendon, be putting yourself out in an effort to be amiable to all. That would be lowering your consequence indeed, and to no purpose.'

The Viscount, while privately considering her to be a tedious woman, full of her own conceit, thought it prudent not to enter into any dispute with her so early in their acquaintance and accepted her judgements with an outward show of complaisance. The entrance of the tea-tray put an end to the game, and Rodney heard, with mounting disbelief, Lady Quendon announce that they kept early and regular hours and that all lights, other than those in bedrooms, were extinguished at ten o'clock.

'No doubt, my lord, you will be tired after your journey and will be glad to seek your bed. The necessity, too, of speaking with so many strange persons on the morrow can prove excessively exhausting, I assure you.'

Nobly, he forbore to tell her that he had withstood many more arduous journeys in his career, and allowed himself to be conducted upstairs before the prescribed hour of darkness to his large, chilly bedchamber. Here he found his valet endeavouring to cheer a dispirited fire.

'The wind being in the north-east, my lord, they tell me in the kitchen that all the chimneys on this side of the house will smoke,' said that individual morosely.

'Parsons, you are an incurable pessimist! Why, what the devil? A warming-pan in my bed!'

'Those sheets are mortal cold, my lord. I suspect them of being Damp!' declared Parsons with the air of one prepared for the worst. 'I understand this to be a building very subject to the whims of the weather.'

'Maybe,' said Rodney, permitting the valet to draw off his Hessians, 'but I cannot suppose the sheets to be so affected!'

'Nonetheless, my lord, I took the liberty of conveying a bottle of brandy hither. I doubt there has been a fire laid in this room since his late lordship's demise.'

'Was this his room then?'

'The very bed in which he breathed his last!' explained Parsons with sombre relish, but his master only laughed and adjured him to keep his blood-chilling anecdotes for the maidservants belowstairs.

Despite his cheerful demeanour, when he had dismissed his gloomy henchman and sat by the now bravely burning fire, sipping more of his predecessor's excellent brandy, the Viscount found himself to be disagreeably cast down by the events of the evening. Though pleasurably surprised by Mr Edgecombe's reception of him, he was of the opinion that that amiable gentleman might well be a deep file and waiting to see how the cat would jump, though it was not perfectly clear how he should be concerned in the way things fell out at Netherdene.

Lord Penston had been heard to deplore the fact that his godson had a tendency to trust all the world until his trust had been proved to be misplaced, but Rodney was no fool nor so ill a judge of character as not to guess when a man might be playing a part. But how could Edgecombe profit by such conduct? Until the present incumbent married and fathered a son, he was still the heir to the title and nothing could be done to break the line of succession. Which brought Rodney back to the consideration that had been troubling him all evening — just what *was* the line of succession?

Promising himself an early visit to the muniment room, he finished off his brandy and, drawing back the heavy drapes that enclosed the bed, was soon snugly ensconced between the sheets. Allowing no fearful reflections upon the bed's previous occupant to disturb him, he was asleep almost before his head had fairly settled into the pillows.

CHAPTER
FOUR

BEING a fair-minded woman, Miss Patience Routledge had to confess that her groom was perfectly right when he warned her that the young chestnut was not fit to be put to the gig.

'Fresh, 'e be,' had warned Chilcot in the lugubrious manner of his kind. 'No, nor rightly broken to the ribbons neither.'

'Well, as old Tad is still limping sadly and I have put off my visit to Saffron Walden until it has assumed an urgency out of all proportion to its importance, I have no choice, have I?' she countered. 'Do not be troubling yourself on my account, Chilcot. I'll give him his head on the way there and that will shake the fidgets out of him. I promise you I'll not frighten him into fits by attempting to take a fly off his ear or anything of that sort!'

Chilcot permitted himself a slightly sour mile which she rightly interpreted as expressing his disbelief at her being able to do any such thing, but obligingly stood back and watched her as she drove smartly out of the yard, holding the chestnut on a tight rein until they had safely rounded the sharp turn into the road. There, with a long straight stretch in front of her and nothing other than a pair of mating blackbirds and one startled rabbit to dispute possession of it, she gave the young horse his head and they sped along in the warm sunshine between freshly green hedgerows and banks starred with wild flowers and the lacy heads of cowparsley.

Miss Routledge held herself to be no mean whip, possessing light hands and being capable of driving her horses to an inch without ever asking more of them than they could perform, but Rufus was a spirited animal, aptly described by Chilcot as 'a prime bit of blood', and she found it no easy thing to allow her thought to stray from the handling of him.

This was particularly unfortunate because she had set great store on being free for most of a day so that she might the more earnestly consider several problems that were disturbing her serenity of mind.

The first and most serious of these problems concerned her charge, Miss Judith Hammerton. Three seasons in London for an heiress of her expectations and one, moreover, who was endowed with far above the ordinary share of beauty, might reasonably be considered sufficient to secure her a husband. Offers she had received in plenty, of that Miss Routledge was quite assured for the rejected suitors had made no secret of their chagrin, but her methods of discouraging unwelcome admirers by explaining in ruthless detail why she considered they should not suit, and touching lightly upon any defects in the aspirant's character in such a way as permanently to blight his hopes, had earned her the reputation of being uncommon hard to please. Now, since her sudden decision to close the house in Bury Street and withdraw to the Essex countryside, there was no saying if she would ever receive another offer. Yet Mr Hammerton's most earnest injunction to Miss Routledge before he had departed for Jamaica the previous year had been that should his daughter wish to remove herself from the social whirl of London then she must be allowed to do so.

'She has no great liking for it,' he had said in his blunt way. 'I'll not deny it is a disappointment to me, but I've given her her chance and if she chooses not to take it, that's her affair. If she is happier away from town then it would be best that she did not contract a fashionable alliance but married some plain country squire — not but that she would soon tire of him if he was too plain!'

Miss Routledge, thinking of one or two simple rustic gentlemen of her acquaintance, and comparing their limited intelligence with Judith's quick understanding, was in full agreement with him. She was also of the opinion that a short time spent at the Old Hall would lead Miss Hammerton to think more kindly of the advantages of town life, but in this supposition she found herself to be greatly mistaken. Everything about the Old Hall, it would seem, was just as it should be — which was as well, since the lease on the house they had occupied in Hampshire had expired, leaving them with no choice of residence other than Bury Street.

Quite why or when Mr Hammerton had come into possession of the Old Hall Miss Routledge did not know, but as he had rarely encouraged either her or his daughter to accompany him on his visits there, she did not trouble herself unduly on that head, having many other things on which to exercise her mind. The chief among these was his prolonged absence from England, during the course of which only two letters had been received from him by Miss Hammerton and one by herself — if letter it could be called, being little more than a list of instructions, which finished up with a recommendation to her not to look for him at any early date and to hope that she and Judith were still rubbing along together.

On this last point she could assure him with perfect sincerity that nothing could be more agreeable than their situation at the Old Hall, which was not so large that it required a host of servants to attend to the simple needs of two ladies, nor so small that it lowered their consequence in the neighbourhood.

Many people had called to offer the customary civilities, a notable exception being Lady Quendon. Whether this regrettable omission arose from the fact of her ladyship being still in black gloves at the time of their arrival, or was brought about by a certain delicacy of feeling which held her back from acknowledging socially a young lady who made no secret of the fact that her father had derived his fortune from his business ventures, Miss Routledge could not be perfectly sure. Certain it was that those ladies with sons of marriageable age were not behindhand with their attentions, nor did they hesitate to denounce Lady Quendon as being top-lofty to a fault, nor to hazard a cattish guess that she stood more in dread of seeing Euphrasia shone down by Judith's beauty than of any ill that might befall her through association with the daughter of a Cit.

At this point in her reflections Miss Routledge was brought to earth with a rude shock. The gig was bowling speedily past a cottage when, from behind its half-open door, there erupted, barking furiously, a large black dog of indeterminate ancestry.

This undesirable creature hurled itself at the chestnut's heels, which behaviour did not commend itself to the high-bred young horse and, before Miss Routledge was fully awake to the danger, he had the bit fairly between his teeth.

The dog, soon tiring of the sport, dropped back and returned home, satisfied that he had played his part in repelling any possible invasion but, in his alarm, the chestnut hardly noticed this desertion. Miss Routledge, uncomfortably aware of a sharp corner ahead of her, debated upon whether to court disaster by feathering the bend as finely as their rapid rate of progress would allow and so mitigate the chances of a head-on collision with any vehicle approaching in the opposite direction, or to take the easier course of sweeping wide around the corner and praying that the road would continue to be as deserted as hitherto.

Before she could arrive at any decision the matter was taken out of her hands by a sudden gust of wind which lifted her bonnet, already set somewhat askew by the chestnut's first violent plunges, straight off her head and cast it into the roadway. Involuntarily, she put up a hand to clutch at it and the agitated Rufus, sensing the momentary lessening of control, took the corner after his own fashion, that is to say much too sharply, catching the nearside wheel on the bank and overturning the whole equipage full in the path of an oncoming curricle and four.

Miss Routledge's last recollection as her head struck the ground with sufficient force to render her insensible was of hooves thrashing the air above her and shouts of alarm emanating from several unknown personages. When consciousness returned to her a few minutes later, the hooves were no longer in evidence nor was any voice to be heard save one, speaking soothing words to her over-enthusiastic steed. She felt an unaccountable reluctance to open her eyes and, after a little consideration, put this down to the fact that her head was very comfortably lodged on a broad shoulder while a strong arm held her secure. Then the owner of these desirable attributes spoke in a tone indicative of excessive irritation.

'Devil take it, Turvey, this is a pretty pickle! To be taking the corner at that pace — she must have been astray in her wits! And with so young a horse, too.'

The voice that had been speaking soothingly to Rufus made reply: 'He is in a fair lather, my lord. No sort of an animal for a lady to be handling,' it added in a severely deprecating way.

Miss Routledge felt that the speaker and her groom would have much in common and longed to be able to explain to him just how it was she had come to be driving the chestnut when the voice over her head spoke again.

'This is what comes of permitting females to drive out unattended. No doubt she is some local farmer's daughter or sister and so accustomed to these roads that she does not give a thought for anyone else using them. Small use ringing a peal over her now, but what's to be done? You cannot leave the horses, the gig wheel is smashed beyond hope, and if you are thinking that I should toss her up into the curricle and drive to the nearest house you are far and wide, let me tell you! I may belong to the Four-in-Hand Club but I cannot aspire to control a team with one hand and support an insensible female with the other!'

'I am *not* insensible!' announced Miss Routledge in tones which, even to her own ears, sounded rather too loud. This statement had the effect of so startling the gentleman supporting her that he all but withdrew his arm but, seeing her eyes still firmly closed, he tightened his hold again.

'Then let me tell you, ma'am, it is a great wonder that you are not!' he informed her. 'I collect you must have struck the road very forcibly for you have a nasty bruise coming up on your forehead.'

Hesitantly she put up a hand and winced as she touched the afflicted spot. 'Oh, dear, what a bump!' she exclaimed involuntarily and opened her eyes to look up into a pair of remarkably fine ones of an indeterminate grey-green hue, the owner of which was regarding her with an air of deep concern.

'You have also,' he went on dispassionately, 'scratched your face, torn your gown and, at the very least, sprained your wrist, though you may well have broken a bone in it.'

This catalogue of accidents made her sensible of the fact that he was supporting her left wrist in his hand and that it was excessively painful.

'It was the dog, you see,' she articulated carefully, feeling that some explanation was due to him. 'Poor Rufus — my horse, is not yet perfectly trained to draw a carriage and the dog alarmed him, jumping out like that from the cottage. Then — then the wind blew my bonnet off and — and I —' She hesitated, not quite certain of how to go on.

'Chose to save your bonnet rather than your neck!' he finished for her, but he was smiling and, even to her upside-down view of him, the smile was a very taking one. 'Now, ma'am, if you will be so good as to give me your direction I will escort you to your home and my groom can lead or ride your horse.'

'No, don't ride him,' she protested faintly. 'He won't care for that, he is very averse to strangers. He — oh, dear! Chilcot will be shown to have been in the right again. It is too tiresome of him!' The gentleman agreed gravely that to be dealing with persons who invariably proved to have been accurate in their prognostications could be a very lowering experience and courteously enquired how she did. 'Oh, famously, I thank you, sir,' she protested, but hardly had she uttered the words than another wave of faintness came over her.

'Damme, she's gone off again! No farmer's daughter here, Turvey. She spoke of a dog coming out of a cottage, that cannot be too far away. I'll lay her down and do you keep an eye on her while I walk back and see if I can summon help.'

She was dimly aware of being picked up and set down again but so great a sense of lassitude had overcome her that she cared for nothing except to be left in peace. Nonetheless, she felt there was something that should be said and forced her confused brain to coherent thought.

'It wasn't poor Rufus's fault,' she declared at last. 'Chilcot did warn me he would be difficult to handle but I had no choice, you see.'

'Now don't you be putting yourself in a pelter, ma'am,' advised Turvey in so much the same sort of tone he had been using to calm Rufus that she was strongly tempted to giggle. 'No sort of blame can be attached to you if the horse took fright. It was very fortunate that his lordship, being a notable whip, was able to avoid you as you lay in the road.'

'His lordship?' she murmured vaguely.

'Lord Penston, ma'am. We was on our way to Netherdene to call on Viscount Quendon.'

'Oh!' she said, then feeling such monosyllable to be an inadequate response to this piece of information, she volunteered, 'I reside at the Old Hall, on the road to Netherdene.'

'So when you are feeling more the thing, ma'am, we can leave you home. I am hopeful we can persuade this lively fellow to trot along with us.'

'I dare say he will do that for he will know he is going to his stable. He — how absurd! I am feeling so stupidly faint again.'

She revived later to find herself being lifted into the curricle by Lord Penston and received her bonnet from his hands. As she raised her left hand to adjust it, she uttered a sharp gasp of pain. Lord Penston, stepping over her to the box-seat, begged her to make no such effort until they should be in a position to judge better of her injury and, ignoring her protests, firmly straightened the bonnet and tied the ribbons under her chin.

'There!' he said with his delightful smile. 'Apart from a little dust, no one would suspect you to be a lady so recently flung from her carriage. And, dare I say, if this very fetching bonnet had been properly secured in the first place perhaps no such accident would have taken place.'

Feeling this admonishment to be well deserved, Miss Routledge hung her head in some confusion and, after a quick glance at her, Lord Penston turned his attention to his horses. 'Right, Turvey, I have 'em. Do you attach the chestnut and we will be on our way. There is no help to be had from that cottage — just one old crone with not half her wits about her and the villainous dog. I have shut him up but there's no saying she has not freed him again.'

Turvey, having tied Rufus to the handrail, swung himself up behind and they proceeded at a gentle trot, Lord Penston keeping a watchful eye upon his lady passenger to satisfy himself that she was maintaining her position. Presently, the cottage having been passed without further incident, he drew up by the side of the road and instructed Turvey to take his seat on the outside of Miss Routledge who, by reason of her injured wrist, was unable to cling to the rail.

'It will be something of a squeeze, ma'am,' he apologized. 'But you seem to me to be in no good case and I would liefer not have you falling into the road again.'

The good sense of this precaution was amply proven by the fact that her next lucid impression was of being lifted down from the curricle while the voices of Jessop and Miss Hammerton were to be heard instructing his lordship where to place her.

'So bantam-witted of me,' she managed to whisper, 'but it doesn't signify, I assure you. A few hours' rest in my room and I shall be as right as a trivet.'

'You will not move from that sofa until Dr Merriman has seen you,' declared Miss Hammerton roundly. 'Jessop, be so good as to send William for him at once.'

'I believe Chilcot has taken it upon himself to do so, miss.' It was clear from the disapproval in the butler's voice that he considered such action to be a great Encroachment on Chilcot's part but Miss Hammerton nodded her approval.

'Good. Now, sir, if you would be so obliging as to take a glass of wine with me — Jessop, the sherry, if you please — perhaps I could learn from you what precisely has taken place.'

Lord Penston, much diverted by the calm commonsense of this beautiful young lady, allowed himself to be divested of his drab riding-coat and sat, sipping his wine, while he recounted how he had come upon Miss Routledge.

'There is an injury to her left wrist,' he explained, 'and I fear she is all about in her head, but your good doctor will be the best judge of that.'

'Yes,' she agreed, waving a vinaigrette under Miss Routledge's nostrils, 'for he *is* a good doctor, quite unlike that odious Dr Abernethy who attends to our ills in London and who would, I have no doubt, inform my dear Miss Patience that her injuries are due to a digestive disorder and recommend a course of blue pills or calomel!'

'Very likely.' Lord Penston had also had dealings with the redoubtable Dr Abernethy. 'You reside for the most part in London, ma'am?'

'I closed our house in Bury Street two months since,' said Miss Hammerton, setting down the vinaigrette and rising to her feet. 'I believe I will join you in a glass of sherry, sir.'

'Allow me, ma'am.'

As he poured her wine there were a dozen questions jostling together in his mind to be asked. The Old Hall might be no more than a gentleman's neat residence, but its furnishings were far above the touch of any gentleman of modest means. Unless he was much mistaken, the richly veneered cabinet in the corner of the elegant small saloon housed as fine a collection of Meissen and Sèvres as ever he had seen, while the bowl standing on a nearby console table was undoubtedly K'ang H'si. He looked up to find her regarding him with an amused gleam in her eye.

'Yes, sir?' she murmured provocatively.

He could not forbear to smile in response. 'Allow me to present myself, ma'am. I am Lord Penston and I am on my way to call upon my godson, Viscount Quendon.'

The effect of this simple statement was quite unexpected. His hostess all but dropped her glass, a vivid flush suffused her cheeks and throat and, in an instant, she was transformed from an assured lady of fashion into a shyly confused girl.

'I — I had heard that Lady Quendon was in hourly anticipation of the Viscount's arrival,' she managed to get out.

'You are acquainted with Lady Quendon, ma'am?' asked Penston, wondering at her discomposure.

'No,' she said, with a gallant assumption of calm. 'Her ladyship has not done us the honour of calling. My name is Hammerton, my lord, Judith Hammerton.'

If she had expected this announcement to occasion surprise on his part she was to be disappointed. Five full years had passed since Lord Penston had first heard the name of Hammerton, nor had he ever discussed that episode again with his godson. Now the first thought that crossed his mind was who this lovely young woman might be and why had not Lady Quendon left her card on so near a neighbour. None of this speculation, however, showed in his face as he replied smoothly.

'My acquaintance with her ladyship is of the slightest, but I had the impression she was a trifle — ah, formal?'

'Full of starch!' said Miss Hammerton, not mincing matters.

'My father being overseas I have no parent to lend me countenance, though a more *convenable* guardian than my dear Miss Patience here could not be imagined.' As she spoke she moved back to the sofa to lay her hand on Miss Routledge's brow, and the expression of affectionate concern on her face reassured Penston, who was beginning to wonder just what manner of *ménage* he had stumbled upon. 'You say you are going to Netherdene, my lord,' she continued, having satisfied herself that Miss Routledge, though not fully sensible, was as comfortable as was possible. 'Are you aware that Lady Quendon has declared this to be an Open Day?' The look of dismay on his face drew a chuckle from her. 'I see you are not! Your godson will find himself excessively occupied doing the pretty to all the local gentry. I had the notion of driving there myself this afternoon. If it pleases you to stay and partake of a nuncheon with me, then I can learn what Dr Merriman has to say about Miss Patience and discover if I may safely leave her for an hour or two.'

'You are too kind, ma'am.' Penston's first instinct was to decline the invitation and be on his way, then his curiosity got the better of him. 'Should Miss — er, Patience's condition permit, I should indeed be glad of your support. Open Days are beyond my experience and I view the prospect with some misgiving.'

'I am persuaded you are very right to do so,' she concurred. 'And the name is Routledge, Miss Patience Routledge, cousin to my Lord Yeovil. Ah, here comes Dr Merriman.'

Lord Penston, who knew Yeovil to be spoken of as a high stickler, was understandably taken aback by this intelligence and, having to revise his first hasty impression of the household, was grateful that the entrance of the doctor made it unnecessary for him to reply.

Dr Merriman, a rosy-cheeked, cheerful little man, made swift examination, tut-tutting over Miss Routledge's sad plight.

'Naught but a nasty sprain,' he declared of her wrist. 'And no bones broken that I can ascertain. Did she complain of pain elsewhere, my lord?' Penston, who had tactfully withdrawn to a window embrasure, assured him that the lady's whole concern seemed to be for her head. 'Ah, yes, a heavy blow. 'Twill ache for a time yet. A James's Powder every four hours should give her ease. She will be best in bed in a darkened room, Miss Hammerton.'

Judith nodded agreement and listened to his further instructions, interposing a question here and there and showing such good sense that Penston found himself regarding her with unmixed approval. An unusual young woman, to be sure! A beauty who, by the look of things, was not short of a penny and was as ready of tongue and sharp of wit as any high-bred lady of the ton. To these attractions must be added the virtues of a ministering angel, though he shrewdly suspected this particular attribute might only be displayed to one she truly held in affection.

Then, while she oversaw the conveying of Miss Routledge upstairs to her room his thought turned to Rodney and how he was conducting himself at his first Open Day.

*   *   *

The Viscount, understandably enough, had not been over-pleased to discover the morning holding out every promise of developing into one of those rare days that herald the glories of high summer, being as warm and sunny as its predecessor had been dull and cheerless.

Lady Quendon claimed that she had known all along how it would be. 'I am excessively sensitive to every whim of the weather,' she explained to Rodney as they stood together in the hall. 'And yestere'en I felt a great upsurge of spirit which could not be laid entirely to your account, Quendon, gratified though I may be to have at last had the pleasure of receiving you here, so that I knew beyond doubt that to-day would prove to be a Successful Event. The gardens here were laid out by Mr Brown, you know, and are justly renowned so that, the day being clement, the greater number of persons will occupy their time in strolling about outside — which, it must be confessed, is the usual practice and one which I am at a loss to account for. Netherdene may not be an ancient building but, I am of the opinion, it is as true an example of a nobleman's residence as is to be seen in these parts. It cannot, I dare say, be allowed to be as fine as Audley

End,' she admitted after a moment's consideration, 'but then the Edgecombes were never ones to put themselves forward by an ostentatious display of wealth.' Rodney was at a loss quite how to respond to this declaration, having been most unfavourably impressed by Netherdene as an example of a nobleman's residence, and her ladyship, not being in expectation of any reply, continued remorselessly. 'If you would be advised by me, Quendon, do not be caught standing here in the hall when the doors are flung open, for then all will press in to shake you by the hand and you will be detained for ever.'

Being for once in full agreement with her, Rodney at once suggested that, as he had not yet had the opportunity of inspecting the gardens, perhaps he might join those doing so without fear of recognition.

'That would be the very thing,' she allowed, 'though I doubt you can preserve your incognito above a few minutes for, depend upon it, everyone will be on the look for you. Jasper!' She summoned Mr Edgecombe who was standing nearby. 'I cannot propose that you accompany Quendon for that would be the most likely circumstance to draw attention to his presence but, if you were to be near at hand to shield him from presumptuous persons, it might answer very well. I shall remain here, as is my custom, and shall merely say, should anyone enquire, that your precise whereabouts are unknown to me.'

Feeling himself to be dismissed Rodney, accompanied by Mr Edgecombe, made his escape through a side-door into the gardens. The latter, observing the slight frown on the Viscount's usually serene countenance, misread its cause.

'You must forgive her ladyship's somewhat high-handed dealing,' he said. 'She has been used to rule the roast here on these occasions for his late lordship invariably locked himself in his business room with a couple or three bottles of port until the last visitor should have gone.'

'I find myself to be remarkably in sympathy with him,' returned Rodney drily. 'But, in spite of her ladyship's belief to the contrary, surely the house can provide few points of interest to the antiquarian?'

'None whatsoever,' replied Mr Edgecombe promptly. 'The

principal dwelling of the family was used to be the Old Hall but this was found not to be sufficiently spacious for his consequence by the late Viscount's father. Apart from a few fine chimneypieces nothing in Netherdene is over fifty years old and, to be truthful, the grounds are in a sad way. Much of old Capability's handsome lay-out has been so neglected or, which to my mind is a sad reflection on his late lordship's judgement, so altered by some fellow not at all up to the trick whom he called in to execute certain designs for him, that I cannot suppose the result to be worthy of serious acclaim.'

'Why,' asked Rodney, giving air to the question that had much vexed him since setting foot in Netherdene, 'does the entire establishment wear such a run-down air? Lord Quendon may have been a pinchpurse but I take it he was no fool. Was he troubled by ill-health in his latter years?'

'His lordship was certainly no fool, but the death of both his sons so embittered him that his interest in maintaining the estate for one who — if you will forgive me — he held in no great esteem, was not profound.'

'My father, you mean?'

'Yes. Of you he knew nothing, of course.'

This disclosure, not unnaturally, put a period to the conversation and presently Mr Edgecombe took himself off, directing Rodney in the way he should go in order to see the best of the grounds before the arrival of numbers of visitors should render this object impracticable.

*   *   *

The Viscount was well content to wander at ease, admiring the fine trees and rare shrubs that still survived despite the encroaching weed and brambles. Then the approach of a large party, which included in its number several young women possessed of unpleasantly high-pitched and penetrating voices, drove him to seek refuge down an overgown track which, after several hundred yards, opened out unexpectedly into a delightful glade in the midst of which was set a most elegant small temple.

As he stood, admiring this charming prospect, there emerged

from another path which he had not at first perceived, none other than his godfather, Lord Penston and, leaning upon his arm, a lovely young woman.

Of the trio there was no doubt the lady showed the least surprise at the encounter. For his part, Rodney could only stand and stare while, once again, a strange sensation of *déjà vu* stole over him. Crisp golden curls showed beneath a flower-trimmed bonnet, while a mischievous twinkle softened the searching regard of a pair of brilliant blue eyes, set deep under delicate, sweeping brows and fringed by heavy dark lashes. Her lips, quivering on the verge of a smile at the gentleman's stupefaction, were sweetly curved, and parting revealed a glimpse of sparkling white teeth.

Lord Penston was the first to break the silence. 'Well met, Rodney!' he hailed him. 'But who would have thought to find you here — and alone! Are you a fugitive? Has your courage failed you?'

'Until this moment, yes!' confessed Rodney, recalled to a sense of what was proper and regarding Lord Penston in some astonishment. 'But you, sir, what brings you to Netherdene?'

'Only the most urgent of business, I can assure you. If I might be private with you for a few moments —' He turned in apology to the lady who responded with a soft laugh.

'Where more private than here?' she said, motioning towards the temple. 'And I shall stand Cerberus for you outside.'

'I beg you, ma'am, to excuse my godfather his lack of conduct,' said Rodney, making his bow, 'and mine in staring in so ill-bred a manner, but I had no expectation of coming upon a temple of Venus, still less of glimpsing its presiding deity.'

Miss Hammerton's smile broadened at the neatly-turned compliment. 'You are very gallant, sir,' she responded calmly, 'but, as I remember, Venus was not given to wearing bonnets — nor, indeed, anything very much!'

'A careless lady in her apparel, to be sure,' he agreed, smiling back at her. Then Lord Penston intervened.

'Ma'am, may I present this graceless scamp, the Viscount Quendon? Rodney, this lady whose acquaintance I have been privileged to make this morning is Miss Judith Hammerton.'

'Good God!' Rodney, in the act of raising the lady's hand to his lips, was transfixed in astonishment. For a long moment grey eyes met blue until she gently withdrew her hand from his clasp.

'So you remember, my lord?' she murmured demurely.

'How could I not?' he breathed.

Lord Penston, who had been staring from one to the other in blank amazement, suddenly clapped a hand to his forehead and cried out in tones of utter dismay: 'Hammerton! Of course! I had forgotten, dolt that I am!'

'Your interest in the affair was of a passing nature,' Rodney reminded him. 'How came you to pick up the threads to-day?'

His godfather enlightened him in a few sentences while the lady stood with eyes modestly downcast, toying with her pagoda-style parasol, and the Viscount seemed unable to tear his eyes away from the enchanting picture she presented. Then the sounds of the vociferous party approaching their retreat caused Miss Hammerton to say urgently: 'Quickly, sirs! If you desire a few moments' privacy, I shall endeavour to fend them off.'

Taking Rodney by the arm, Lord Penston hurried him into the little building, while their self-appointed guardian, opening up her parasol, perambulated gracefully to and fro upon the grass as if in deep meditation.

Rodney, not unreasonably mystified by his godfather's portentous air, begged to be informed as to its cause.

'To be brief, I received a letter yesterday from Sir Charles Stuart in Paris. He advises that you do not pursue further your enquiries about your father's disappearance.'

'Why should I not?'

'Because, though he phrases it as delicately as possible, it is clear that Sir Rollo had been engaged in — er, dubious activities for some years past. His reappearance could prove embarrassing.'

'D'you mean he was smuggling? I have always suspected that! But, great Heaven! If everyone who ever contrived to outwit the excisemen was obliged to flee the country, England would be deprived of half her population!'

'It is not precisely a matter of outwitting the excisemen.'

The gravity of Lord Penston's expression made Rodney exclaim sharply: 'What is it, then, sir? You seem to hint at some more heinous crime.'

'Betrayal of one's country's secrets is indeed a heinous crime.'

'You cannot mean — I won't believe it!' Rodney's flushed cheek and flashing eyes bore witness to his rising choler. Lord Penston laid a restraining hand on his shoulder.

'Believe me, my dear boy, when I say I am as horrified as you. God knows your father was no friend of mine, he was a gamester and a rake, but never would I have suspected him of being a traitor.'

'How can you be sure of this?'

'I collect Sir Charles has adequate proof. For your sake, none of this will be made known unless your father is found to be alive.'

'But why? In God's name, why?' The anguish in the young voice affected Penston deeply but he was careful to keep his tone flatly matter-of-fact when replying.

'For money, I should suppose. After your mother died there was no restraint upon his spending. His way of life was beyond reason extravagant. Now, do not be refining too much upon this, Rodney. You owe him nothing and if he is guilty of these charges he'll stay hid.'

'But, sir, he is my father! He may be destitute.'

'I dare swear he is not!' retorted Penston grimly. 'To my way of thinking Sir Rollo, fearful of the outcome of the battle at Waterloo and knowing himself to be ruined if the Allies won, took the precaution of disappearing before any could point an accusing finger at him. Had Bonaparte proved triumphant then he would have emerged from hiding to claim his blood-money of which, I have no doubt, he has plenty hid away to be on the safe side of chance.'

'So you believe him to be alive?'

'I do.'

'Could my mother have known of this?' asked Rodney unexpectedly. 'Could it have been the cause of their estrangement?'

'Ask yourself,' said his godfather gently, 'if your mother

would have put loyalty to such a husband before loyalty to her country?'

'I think so — if she loved him.' Rodney spoke half to himself. 'Women see these things differently. To them duty and honour are words to be painted on a large canvas, their first consideration is the smaller span of the domestic scene.'

Penston raised an eyebrow in surprise at this knowledgeable dissertation on the gentler sex. 'If your mother had suspected any of this,' he said slowly, 'I truly believe she would have told me. Put that notion from you, Rodney. Whatever the cause of the rift between your parents, it was not this.'

The murmur of voices outside their retreat caused both gentlemen to stand silent while Miss Hammerton could be heard explaining that she was placed there on guard to prevent anyone from entering the temple.

'The flooring is none too safe,' she elaborated. 'I would strongly advise against putting foot on it. This unfortunate circumstance was only discovered yesterday so there has been no time to remedy the defect.' A man's voice was heard to say something and she replied. 'Yes, sir, a most happy chance else some unwary visitor must surely have broken a limb.'

'A ready tongue!' remarked Lord Penston softly. 'And — by Jupiter! Her father was well known to yours. He is in Jamaica now, she tells me, since last July. Could it be —?'

'That my father is with him? Would she know?'

'Possibly not. And it would be best not to enquire too closely.'

Rodney shook his head decisively. 'No, sir, it won't do. I must know the truth. Believe me, I am not throwing the hatchet when I say that I have often wished you were my father rather than he who is, but I am his son and if there is a chance that this story is untrue then I must do my utmost to disprove it.'

'You may well make things worse,' warned Penston. 'For if any of this should come out then the whole must be made public.'

'That I know but — you do understand, sir?' He held out his hand and his godfather clasped it strongly.

'I would feel the same in your place,' he admitted.

'Then I am persuaded we should cultivate the acquaintance of these ladies,' pursued Rodney thoughtfully. 'When does Miss Hammerton anticipate her father's return to England?'

'She made no mention of it.' Penston raised his head to listen for a moment. 'Perhaps we had better relieve her of her duties, it sounds as if she is being subjected to question yet again. She is,' he added, 'a very unusual young woman.'

'She is a very handsome one,' amended Rodney, smiling faintly, but the smile hardened perceptibly as they stepped out into the sunshine and he perceived that Miss Hammerton's companion was Mr Jasper Edgecombe. She greeted them with her lovely smile and Rodney was so taken by its charm that he quite failed to observe Lord Penston's start of astonishment when Mr Edgecombe swung round to face him.

'I see there is no need for me to present you to Miss Hammerton, gentlemen, though I am desolated to learn of the cause of your meeting her. Miss Routledge has taken no lasting hurt, I hope?'

Miss Hammerton assured him that she had every expectation of Miss Routledge being quite recovered in a few days and made him known to Lord Penston. Thereupon the four strolled on through the grounds, encountering numerous parties of visitors who glanced at them curiously, many bowing to Mr Edgecombe and some few to Miss Hammerton, but none venturing to detain them. When they had arrived near to the house a footman approached them with a request from the dowager that Lord Quendon should attend her. Rodney at once suggested that the whole party join her ladyship, but Miss Hammerton begged to be excused, saying she would prefer to take a further turn in the garden since her time was limited by the necessity of returning to Miss Routledge's side before that lady took the notion of rising from her bed.

'Which, be assured, she will do at the first possible moment, despite Dr Merriman's warnings.'

Mr Edgecombe, too, excused himself on the score of having to consult with the gatekeeper on the number of persons admitted to the grounds during the afternoon.

'For if we do not account for every one it goes without saying that someone will get shut in when we close the gates.'

It occured to Lord Penston to wonder as he watched the tall, well-set-up figure walking steadily away, whether Mr Edgecombe might not wish Lady Quendon to know of his friendship with Miss Hammerton, but he had no time to ponder this interesting possibility as Rodney, refusing to accept her excuses, had taken Judith's arm and was escorting her up the steps and into the hall.

'A matter of moments only,' he promised her, 'and as you say you have not made Lady Quendon's acquaintance, what better time than now?'

'But,' she protested, 'her ladyship may not be of the same mind and it does appear as if I am forcing myself upon her in her own house.'

'My house! he corrected her. 'And while I'll not indulge in a panegyric on her disposition, I promise you she don't actually bite!'

She had to smile at that but the dowager's icy stare, which became even more glacial when she understood who was the lady on the Viscount's arm, speedily restored her to sobriety. Sitting with her ladyship was Miss Edgecombe, whose eyes opened very wide indeed as they took in the interesting contrast of Miss Hammerton's golden beauty beside Rodney's dark good looks.

The dowager, however affronted she might feel at having to acknowledge Miss Hammerton's existence, put up a good show of civility but stressed her disapproval of having such acquaintance thrust upon her by turning to greet Lord Penston with the utmost affability. He lost no time in recounting his adventures of the day and she, in an excess of hospitality, begged him to regard Netherdene as his particular property and to stay for as long as he wished. He protested that he had no notion of putting her to any such inconvenience and that he had no doubt of the Sun at Saffron Walden being able to accommodate him for the night.

'I assure you, my lord, it will not cause me the least inconvenience,' said Lady Quendon with perfect truth. 'Euphrasia, instruct Brough to see that a bedchamber is made ready for his lordship.'

Some other favoured persons then joined the group and it was not for several minutes that Rodney noticed Miss Hammerton was no longer with them. Murmuring an excuse, he stepped to the open door and scanned the numerous groups of visitors promenading about on the gravel paths. He was rewarded by a glimpse of her lilac dress and parasol disappearing behind a shrubbery of laurel and had no doubt that the gentleman escorting her was Mr Edgecombe. Again, he felt the most unwarranted surge of resentment and was about to step forward in pursuit of them when Penston's hand on his arm restrained him.

'An odd coincidence, to be sure,' said that gentleman, plucking at his lower lip with finger and thumb as was his wont when perplexed.

'Meeting Miss Hammerton again, d'you mean?'

'That as well, but it was your cousin Jasper of whom I was thinking.'

Rodney looked at him quickly. 'Indeed, sir?'

Penston raised a quizzical eyebrow. 'You must have observed the resemblance?'

'Yes,' allowed Rodney, 'he puts me most strongly in mind of some other.'

'I should rather think he might! He is the finished likeness of your father — your father as he was twenty-five years ago, of course. Sir Rollo has changed greatly, or had when last I saw him, but the resemblance is undeniable, even to gestures and turns of speech.'

Rodney began to dispute this assertion then, as the truth of it came home to him, he asked casually: 'In what way is Jasper Edgecombe related to me?'

Lord Penston, undeceived by his godson's idle manner, helped himself to snuff and replaced the fine enamelled box in his pocket before replying.

'His mother was second cousin to the late Viscount and she married an even more distant cousin, or so I understand it.'

'Then Jasper is doubly an Edgecombe?'

'That doesn't signify. You are no less so because your grandfather took the name of Nairn when your grandmother came into her family's fortune.'

'I'll wager he did that out of a fit of pique rather than a wish to oblige his wife's family!'

Penston laughed. 'Anything to put his brother out of countenance, I dare say! And do not ask me what *that* right royal quarrel was all about but it appears to have been maintained by their sons.'

'To the extent of the late Viscount allowing his estates to fall into disrepair in order to spite my father.'

'Indeed? I can well believe it. An irascible tribe, the Edgecombes.' Penston raised his quizzing-glass the better to inspect the animated scene before him. 'If her ladyship is agreeable, I think I may extend my stay here by a few days. The future holds promise of some interest.'

I would be much in your debt if you could do so,' returned Rodney warmly. 'For the prospect of enduring another such evening as I was obliged to spend last night is enough to make me contemplate removal to Bedlam with perfect equanimity.'

'As bad as that? Then to preserve your sanity, I must certainly remain with you a little longer. Come, we must appear somewhat particular, standing thus apart. It will never do for you to be spoken of as a haughty sort of man, too stiff-necked to do the civil by your neighbours.'

As such an accusation would have been abhorrent to him, Rodney made no demur, and they stepped back into the hall to rejoin the group around the dowager, though his thoughts still lingered with a certain young lady in lilac and his undoubtedly beguiling cousin, Mr Jasper Edgecombe.

CHAPTER
FIVE

'YOU don't tell me that you had no notion of the identity of the new Viscount Quendon?' accused Miss Routledge.

'Certainly I had,' returned Miss Hammerton coolly. 'Could you, of your kindness, Miss Patience, inform me of the best way to clean this white ostrich feather? It has gone sadly yellow.'

'White soap, cut small, dissolved in hot water and beaten to a lather,' said Miss Routledge promptly, and returned to the attack. 'When your father purchased this house was it because he had the intention of espousing you to Mr Nairn and thought the Old Hall conveniently situated to Netherdene for the purpose should Mr Nairn succeed to the title?'

'How can I hazard a guess at what was in my father's mind all that time ago?' countered Miss Hammerton. 'White soap beaten to a lather, you say, and then?'

'Dip the ostrich feather in and out for several minutes, then rinse it in very hot water. After than, a final cool rinse and shake it near the fire to dry.'

It was the second day following Miss Routledge's unfortunate mishap and, declaring herself to be perfectly stout in health, she was reclining on a sofa in the saloon, clad in a modish confection of bronze satin, masquerading under the name of dressing-robe, which had been Miss Hammerton's Christmas gift to her. On her gleaming brown curls was placed the daintiest imaginable cap of Mechlin lace, and the picture she presented was so captivating that it was difficult to believe she was a lady whose thirtieth birthday lay only weeks ahead. She was also a lady who was resolved to have the truth of Miss Hammerton's behaviour.

'Then — correct me if I am in error,' she went on slowly, 'can this be the reason for your closing the house in Bury Street and coming to live here? You knew his lordship must come to

Netherdene to claim his inheritance, you — Judith! You have never forgotten him, have you?'

Miss Hammerton, seated at a handsome double-sided writing table, was seemingly absorbed in setting down the directions for cleaning white ostrich feathers in her household book, and made no direct reply to this accusation but, dipping her quill into the richly gilded Worcester inkstand, said: 'Did you know this taperstick was cracked? It must have suffered damage during the journey from Bury Street.'

She was dressed in a crisp blue cotton frock, with a snug-fitting white silk spenceret that left her graceful throat and neck bare save for a thin gold chain. Miss Routledge, watching her, was filled with a sense of awe. For so young a girl to display such tenacity of purpose came as a revelation even to her, who was well acquainted with her charge's strength of character. She was about to comment further on so interesting a situation when Jessop entered the room to inform the ladies that Lord Penston and the Viscount Quendon had called to enquire after Miss Routledge's well-being.

'I have taken the precaution of showing the gentlemen into the book-room, miss, not knowing if you would be wishful to receive them.'

'Of course she would,' said Miss Hammerton briskly. Miss Routledge looked imploringly at her but she only laughed. 'It is very civil of them to call and you must thank Lord Penston for his good offices in rescuing you. Please to announce them, Jessop.'

Swiftly she threw a soft rug over Miss Routlege's knees and moved into the centre of the room, smoothing out her skirts and glancing critically at her appearance in the large pier-glass set between the windows.

'It is all very well, Judith,' protested Miss Routledge, 'but you are in your best looks and got up very handsomely, too.'

'So are you got up very handsomely, Miss Patience,' retorted Miss Hammerton, patting an errant curl into position and stepping forward in welcome as Jessop ushered in the two gentlemen.

'You disappeared so mysteriously from Netherdene t'other

day, ma'am, that had yesterday not been taken up with necessary duties, I must have called to enquire in what way I — we had earned your displeasure.'

Thus Rodney, and Miss Routledge, watching him kiss Judith's hand with easy grace, thought that the years had dealt uncommonly kindly with young Mr Nairn. Then Lord Penston was by her side, enquiring how she did.

'It is plain to be seen that you are in much better case than when last we met, ma'am, though that tiresome bruise on your forehead tells its own story.'

'Oh, sir, what you must have thought of me that day beggars description!' she sighed, pleasurably relieved to find that her memory had not played her false and that he was as manly and elegant in form, and with as charming a smile, as she had imagined him to be. For his part, Penston could not comprehend why he had not perceived at their first meeting that she was a most distinguished-looking female — a handsome one, too, with delicate features and a pronounced air of quality. Her hazel eyes sparkled with humour as she informed him that, even if she was not yet quite up to snuff, she was not thought to be in general a vapourish female, despite her deplorable behaviour of two days before. 'Indeed, my lord, you must have rated my conduct to have been foolish beyond permission.'

He assured her that her behaviour had been entirely consistent with that of a lady who had received a stunning blow on the head, then, as he turned to greet Miss Hammerton, Rodney took his place, smiling down upon her and protesting she must have quite forgotten him.

'Yes, you have the advantage of me there,' put in his godfather. 'I had not the felicity of making these ladies' acquaintance five years ago.'

'And my meeting with them was all too brief,' said Rodney ruefully. 'Have you ever forgiven me, I wonder? My incivility, my gauche dismissal of myself — why your father did not order me to be thrown into the street, I shall never know! Gad! What a chawbacon I must have appeared to him!'

'You did not to me,' Miss Routledge assured him. 'Just young and engagingly innocent.'

'Well, they say the Lord gives years but the Devil gives increase!' said Lord Penston cheerfully, drawing up a stool by the sofa as Miss Routledge gestured to them to be seated. Rodney, setting a chair for Miss Hammerton, politely enquired when she could expect to see her father again.

'Why, it was only yesterday I had a letter from him, informing me that most likely before I had received it, he would be in Portugal. That, at least, is some degree nearer home than Jamaica.'

Rodney hesitated, then, seeing the other two deep in conversation, decided to hazard all on one throw of the dice. 'Is it possible, do you suppose, that your father could have some knowledge about the disappearance of mine?' he asked quietly. She turned her head to regard him steadily.

'I suspect it to be very possible, my lord,' she replied. 'But I question if what he had to tell you would be to your liking.'

'I don't take your meaning, ma'am.' The quick resentment in his voice betrayed him and her keen gaze softened as she went on in a low voice.

'My father, I would have you know, my lord, is no petty shop-keeper. He deals in large commodities and has agents placed all over Europe to procure his requirements. I do not know what was the precise connection between him and Sir Rollo.' She paused, uncertain of how to phrase her suspicions without offending him.

'My father could have been one of those agents?'

'And one, perhaps, who provided a — a commodity outside the law?'

He laughed shortly. 'His smuggling activities would scarcely account for his disappearance, ma'am.'

'What are you thinking, my lord?'

'I hardly know,' he confessed, and the troubled look in his clear eyes came near to oversetting her composure, but further discussion was denied them for Lord Penston was rallying them on their low-voiced exchange which, he declared, gave all the appearance of secrecy.

Then the conversation turned to the Second Spring Meeting at Newmarket and how indifferently Lord Penston's colt had performed over the Rowley Mile. He was gratified to learn of Miss Routledge's interest in horse-racing and was proceeding to expand upon this favoured subject when Mr Jasper Edgecombe was announced. That gentleman showed no surprise at the presence of the other two visitors having, as he explained, observed Lord Penston's curricle in the yard.

'We are all, I make no doubt, here upon the same errand,' he remarked. 'To enquire how our dear Miss Patience goes on.'

His dear Miss Patience was strongly tempted to inform him that she had not, as far as her memory led her to believe, granted him the right to use her given name, but she repressed so ignoble an impulse and greeted him with her usual serenity. There was no reason in the world why she should distrust Mr Edgecombe, but the plain fact was that she did, nor could she understand Judith's being partial to his company.

Lord Penston, while allowing it to be most unfair, had also taken the gentleman in aversion. Edgecombe, after all, was hardly to be blamed in that he bore a strong resemblance to Sir Rollo. Apart from that one failing, his manners were impeccable and his attitude to the Viscount all that it should be, combining as it did, affability and deference in nice proportions. Miss Routledge's voice recalled his lordship to a sense of the present before he had time to consider just why he suspected Mr Edgecombe of being other than perfectly amiable.

That gentleman was conveying to Rodney a message that had come in from one of the outlying farms about damage to the main roof of the farmhouse. 'It is a matter of a tie-beam giving way, which in its turn has affected the collars and rafters — do not ask me to be more precise, I am no house-builder, but it sounded to be urgent. As Sowerby, your agent, set off early this morning to attend to some flooding in the Low Meadows, I thought it prudent to send the carpenter to Eltham Farm and follow him up to judge of the damage for myself. It is some eight miles distant from here,' he added, 'and so doubly an excuse for calling on these charming ladies.'

'I had thought to visit there to-morrow,' said Rodney slowly. 'Perhaps if I went to-day?' He looked in question at Mr Edgecombe who nodded briskly.

'It would answer very well,' he agreed. 'If you will be pleased to ride my Trumpeter you can cut close on two miles off the way and maybé take in Chedwell Farm on your return.'

'Now that,' put in Miss Hammerton, 'is a building worthy of your attention, being a moated farmhouse, of which we have many in these parts. Chedwell, however, is most exceptional in its state of preservation.'

'Why a moat?' asked the mystified Viscount.

'Because of the wolves!' she informed him and had to laugh at his look of consternation.

'That may have been the case at one time, but I'd wager no one has seen a wolf in these parts for a century or more,' Mr Edgecombe assured him.

'Then I had best be on my way and am grateful to you for sending the carpenter in advance of me, for I warrant I know even less about roofs than you!' Rodney then took his leave of the ladies and advised Lord Penston of the change in their arrangements. 'I would be happy if you could carry Edgecombe back to Netherdene in my place and convey my apologies to her ladyship. With two such calls to make I doubt I'll be back before mid-afternoon.'

'You do know the way, I presume?' asked his godfather.

'To Eltham Farm — yes, I studied it on the estate map this morning, but from Chedwell I am not so sure.'

'You can go by the lanes,' interposed Mr Edgecombe. 'Or require the farmer to guide you through his fields and then by a bridle-path to the Home Wood. Once there, you may gallop down the Long Stretch and be at Netherdene in little over half an hour. The lanes, being somewhat tortuous, take longer but Trumpeter knows them well, for I often use that way when coming over from Thaxted, so you'll not likely get lost.'

'Benighted and surrounded by ravening wolves!' murmured Miss Hammerton in mock dismay. Rodney, who had encountered these savage creatures in the Pyrenees, barely repressed a shudder.

'Rest assured if you have not returned by dinner time we will come in search of you!' promised Lord Penston and, amid such cheerful banter, the gentlemen took their leave, promising themselves the pleasure of calling again at no very distant date.

It was close on an hour later and the ladies had just partaken of a light nuncheon, that Jessop announced the arrival of yet another visitor.

'A Miss Cartwright,' he said, looking to be quite shaken out of his customary calm. 'A foreign-seeming lady by her dress and — and Accoutrements.'

'Accoutrements? What can you mean, Jessop?' Miss Routledge asked of him. 'You make her sound like a cavalry officer, all clanking sword and gleaming spurs!'

'Not at all like a cavalry officer, miss!' Jessop declared, and was proceeding to elaborate when a clear resonant voice from the doorway broke in upon his explanations.

'Indeed, I should hope not, though they are dashing fellows, to be sure! Judith, my dear, have you so soon forgotten your old friend?'

'Georgiana Cartwright! Indeed I have not forgotten you!' Miss Hammerton rose and ran with outstretched arms to welcome the newcomer. 'But I had not imagined you to be in England.'

While the two young women embraced and exchanged delighted greetings, Miss Routledge had ample opportunity of observing Miss Cartwright, a tall girl in her twenties, built on Junoesque lines, and dressed in the very first style of fashion. Her magnificent chestnut hair was piled on top of her head with no concession to curls or fringes; her complexion was un-ashamedly sunbrowned; her nose unremarkable; only her sparkling dark eyes and generous mouth distinguished her countenance. Despite her undeniable lack of all pretension to beauty, there was a glowing radiance about her that made every gentleman she encountered look twice at her — and every lady, too, though doubtless for different reasons.

'Miss Patience! But how delightful to meet you again!' said this redoubtable young lady, stepping up to the sofa. 'But how is this? You are not feeling quite the thing?'

While she reassured her visitor on this point, Miss Routledge reflected that Georgiana Cartwright had changed little in the three years since they last had met. That had been on the

occasion of Judith's come-out in London and the older girl had
been kindness itself, caring not a fig that her protégée was a
tearing beauty who might be expected to shine her down.

The friendship between the two young women had been
prematurely disrupted when Sir Humphrey Cartwright had
departed for Lisbon to join General Sir Warren Peacocke's staff,
taking his daughter with him to act as his hostess.

'But, Georgiana, what felicity to see you!' Judith was in rare
transports of delight. 'How does it come about? Shall you stay
awhile with us? Is there aught we can do for your comfort?'

'Indeed there is!' replied Miss Cartwright, undismayed by
this torrent of questions. 'You can house me and my possessions
for a few days, if you would be so kind.'

Miss Routledge looked at Jessop who had remained by the
door in a pose of stiff disapproval. 'Request Mrs Searle to have a
room prepared for Miss Cartwright at once, if you please.'

'Yes, miss. What does the young lady wish to have done with
her carriage and the wagon?'

'The wagon?' asked the fascinated Miss Routledge.

'Oh, do not be troubling your head about that!' Miss
Cartwright waved the wagon aside. 'It is one of Pickford's. If you
don't care for it they will take it away until I am ready for it to be
sent to Bishop's Stortford. But may I beg shelter for my carriage?
The postboys can take the team back later.'

'Jessop, see to it, please.'

The butler bowed and withdrew, but not before casting a very
speaking glance at Miss Routledge, who could not help but be
diverted by his gloomy mien. His gloom was further increased
when, on returning to the kitchen quarters, he found that a
groom and a maid had also materialized which Miss Cartwright
had not thought to mention, at which point he relinquished all
responsibility and went out to deal with the postboys.

Judith suggested that Miss Cartwright would like to refresh
herself and partake of some food, but that young woman
declined any such mundane considerations and disposed herself
on the nearest vacant chair, stretching out her long legs with a
sigh of contentment.

'No, I thank you, not until I have acquainted you with the

reason for this descent upon you. First you must know that my father is being despatched back to England. He and I were to have made the journey in advance of my mother so that I might put his house, Fairacre, which lies on the farther side of Bishop's Stortford from here, to rights before her arrival. Yes,' she nodded in response to Judith's exclamation of surprise, 'she is my stepmother. My father married again, early this year, a Portuguese lady who has never set foot in England and does not view the prospect with any great degree of relish. I told my father how it would be, but he insists that she gives it a run. Myself, I consider it would be better if she remained in Lisbon until he can contrive to get himself sent back there — a thing not at all beyond his powers. I cannot be sure, but you never did meet Sir Humphrey, did you? He holds London and the beau monde quite in abhorrence and I well remember his depositing me upon my aunt's doorstep for the season and springing back into the carriage with a cry of: "Play your cards well, my girl! I'll give my consent to any reasonable proposal!" However, that is beside the point. The cause of my present difficulty is that my father was unavoidably detained on the very day we were to leave Lisbon and, as everything had been put in train for the journey, I could do no other than proceed without him. By good fortune, some friends were returning to England at the same time and I came in their company. They, however, were going to Brighton and so we parted at Dover and I went to London to seek lodging with my aunt, only to find her out of town and the house shut up.'

The door opened once again to admit a scandalized Jessop.

'What will you wish done with the parrot, miss?' he enquired in a tone which made very clear that such Domestic Appendages were not at all what he was accustomed to nor approved of.

'Keep his cage covered, if you please, and leave it in the carriage. He belongs to my father,' she explained to the other two ladies. 'He was purchased from a sailor in Lisbon and his vocabulary is not at all suited to a drawing-room. Where was I? Oh, yes. Finding my aunt out of town — we had no means of warning her of my arrival, you see, for had my father been with me we would have gone to the Clarendon. The very notion of staying with any of his relatives does not commend itself to him, he declares them all to be dull beyond permission — I went at once to Bury Street in search of you, only to find it closed, but your porter gave me your direction.'

'How — how clever of you to remember the exact house in Bury Street,' Miss Routledge managed to say.

'I might not have recalled the precise location,' admitted Miss Cartwright, 'had not Mr Hammerton refreshed my memory.'

'What? You have seen my father? But where?'

'At Lisbon, to be sure, just before I left. He has charged me with all manner of messages for you and promises himself the felicity of being with you before many days are past. Oh, one thing more. You father bid me to be most particular to ask you if Viscount Quendon has come to claim his inheritance.'

'Why, yes, he was here but an hour since with his godfather, Lord Penston,' said the surprised Miss Routledge. 'Do you know him, then?'

'Yes, indeed. While in Lisbon my father kept open house for any wounded officers or those who could snatch a short respite from their arduous duties in Spain. Captain Nairn was a month with us upon one occasion — of excellent address, is he not? I'll warrant all the mamas of marriageable daughters will be filled with interest when he goes upon the strut in London! Which puts me in mind of what I would ask — how does it come about that you are still unwed, my fair Judith? I had supposed you to be soundly established by now with a couple of hopeful brats to your credit!'

'Reflect, Georgy, that we once drew up a list of qualities which we deemed to be essential in our future husbands!' Miss Hammerton reminded her friend.

'And you have met no gentleman to match up to these demands? I cannot believe it possible!' The twinkle in Miss Cartwright's eye belied her words. 'Can you be growing a little too nice in your requirements?'

'No more than you it would seem! For I perceive no wedding band upon your finger either!' retorted Miss Hammerton.

'That is all about to be changed,' announced Miss Cartwright. 'For now that my father has married again he has no need of me —

oh, mistake me not, my new mama is of a most kindly and obliging disposition. She is also excessively indolent and were I to remain in her household would gladly leave the charge of it in my hands. But I have a mind for an establishment of my own, for I am now twenty-four years of age and will soon be on the shelf if I do not make a push to attach some gentleman.'

'But, surely, it is for your father or some female relative —' began Miss Routledge weakly.

'Not a chance in the world!' stated Miss Cartwright cheerfully. 'I am not regularly handsome nor distinguished for elegant accomplishments and, though I am possessed of a very reasonable competence from my mother, my father declares I am too hot at hand to make anyone a complaisant wife, so he washes his hands of me, while my aunt and I, as has been proven before, would be altogether by the ears inside an hour. I suspect you, Judith, are cast in the same mould, too independent of spirit to be generally pleasing. What is to be done with us? Shall we set up house together like Lady Eleanor Butler and Miss Ponsonby, here in Essex?'

'No, I am persuaded that would not answer,' said Judith, shaking her head. 'In any case, I have other plans.'

'Your father rather thought you might!' Miss Cartwright was looking mischievous. 'Now, tell me, apart from Quendon, what other eligible gentlemen are to be found hereabouts?'

'Georgy, you are incorrigible!' Laughing, Judith arose. 'Come, let me show you to your room and discover how my staff have dealt with your — your Accoutrements!'

Left to herself, Miss Routledge meditated on this unexpected turn of events. Such a large pebble as Georgiana Cartwright dropped into the small pool of their existence at the Old Hall was bound to make something of a splash. She only hoped Miss Cartwright did not plan to cast her matrimonial net over Quendon else the friendship between the young ladies might become a trifle strained. Then she gave herself up to contented musings, not unconnected with a pair of fine grey-green eyes and a delightful smile, for which she presently took herself to task. Such presumption in a mere companion was not to be thought on. Lord Penston's attentions were no more than the customary civilities to be expected of so well-bred a gentleman and it was ridiculous to refine too much upon them.

Thereupon she applied herself to perusing the *Ipswich Journal* and was gratified to learn from that undoubted arbiter of fashion that the jacket and petticoat were coming strongly into vogue, the jacket being fastened in front over the petticoat fastened behind. But when Judith and Georgiana, having exhausted their confidences, came down to drink tea with her, they found her nodding gently, the *Ipswich Journal* fallen unheeded to the floor, and smiling as if at some undisclosed happy memory.

CHAPTER
SIX

RODNEY experienced no difficulty in discovering his way to
Eltham Farm and listened with becoming gravity to all the
carpenter had to tell him concerning the faulty roof. Admittedly,
he was no wiser after this dissertation than before for, in addition
to the incomprehensible terms of his trade, the old man spoke
with a strong local accent and used expressions quite foreign to
the Viscount, who had prided himself on knowing something of
the Essex dialect.

'Shall you finish to-day?' he enquired.

'Na, but I'll give ut a good shak'n!' he was assured and went on
his way, chuckling and vowing to take his agent along with him
on all such visits in the future.

Chedwell Farm proved to be as interesting as Miss
Hammerton had declared it to be and the farmer's wife did
justice to the occasion by producing a most potent brew of
elderberry wine which, had it not been accompanied by huffkins,
a kind of cake thought highly of in her native Kent, must surely
have sent her landlord on his way a trifle disguised. As it was, the
afternoon was well advanced before he threw leg over
Trumpeter again and bade farewell to his host and hostess.

'Ye cannot miss the way, my lord. Follow down by the side o'
th' fields, 'tis cappy soil and ye can box along ut. Then afront ye
will be th' spurway. Turn west and in half-a-mile ye'll be at th'
Home Wood.' Rodney gratefully recognized 'spurway' to mean
bridle-path and nodded his understanding as the farmer went on:
'Ye ain't no call to be a-scriggl'n thro' th' lanes — one false turn
and ye'll be back where ye started. Matt! Mount th' cob and set
his lordship on't way.'

The grinning Matt would have been more than ready to ride
with him to Netherdene, but Rodney, suspecting that the farmer

had a better use for him, despatched him back to Chedwell as they entered the Home Wood. Then he cantered on alone at an easy pace until he came to the Long Stretch, an inviting two miles of undulating greensward with the trees crowding closely upon it on either side.

'What d'you say, old fellow?' he murmured into Trumpeter's cocked ear. 'I warrant you'd be glad of the chance to exercise your legs — off with you!'

Immediately the big horse gathered his haunches under him and bounded away. Rodney gave him his head, praying there were no rabbit holes lying in wait for an unwary hoof, and they flew down the green ribbon of grass, at no point more than thirty feet wide. At the end Trumpeter, though by no means distressed, stood for a moment with heaving flanks then advanced again towards the trees. In so doing, he stumbled over a hidden tree-root and Rodney, taken unaware, was jolted slightly forward. A shot rang out from no great distance away and, almost simultaneously, he experienced a stinging blow to the upper part of his left arm. Realizing at once that he had been hit, he reined in Trumpeter and slid off his back.

'Hey, there!' he called indignantly. 'Watch your aim! I'm no sitting pigeon for your sport!'

Silence greeted his protest, a silence so complete that Rodney presumed the marksman to be either stunned with horror at what he had done, or to be stealing furtively away from the scene lest he should be called to account for his action.

Securing Trumpeter to the branch of a strong young oak, Rodney pulled down the shoulder of his riding-coat to inspect the damage. The bullet had struck his upper forearm on the inside and it required no great effort of the imagination to understand that had the horse not stumbled when he did, that bullet could well have lodged in his heart. The wound was bleeding profusely so that he was at a loss to know how to check it and, making a rough pad of his handkerchief, he resolved to waste no time in getting back to Netherdene.

Trumpeter who, understandably enough, had taken strong exception to the noise of the shot, needed little urging to be on his way, making it plain that he held no good opinion of persons who discharged their firearms in so liberal a fashion. After they had covered a mile or so at a steady pace, Rodney was brought to the realization that he had quite lost his direction, but as his mount was moving confidently along a well-worn track he concluded that the animal knew what he was about and gave him his head.

His faith was justified when presently the trees thinned out and they emerged from the wood to stand upon a slight eminence. Below them lay the Old Hall amid its formal gardens, with nearby flint and brick church, topped by a wooden belfry, and the village cottages set at a proper distance from their betters. The house, Rodney recalled rather hazily, had been the Edgecombes' old home before they had aspired to the bleak grandeur of Netherdene. This proved to be his last coherent thought for some time for Hall, church, and landscape all combined to revolve around him in the most disturbing manner and, in endeavouring to dismount, he fell to the ground in a dead faint.

Trumpeter nosed the crumpled form of his rider in question but, meeting with no response, very sensibly went on his way. As he entered the stableyard with all the assurance of a frequent visitor in no doubt of his cordial reception, he encounterd two ladies just about to ride out, Miss Hammerton on her spritely bay mare and Miss Cartwright on a handsome black who rolled a nervous eye at the new arrival. Chilcot, who was standing hands on hips watching them depart, uttered an exclamation and sprang to seize Trumpeter's reins.

''Tis Mr Edgecombe's mount —'

'My lord Quendon rode off on him this morning!' Judith's cheeks were as white as the lace at her throat.

'There's blood on the saddle, miss!' In an instant Chilcot had mounted the indignant Trumpeter and was turning him back the way he had come.

'Chedwell — the Home Wood!' Judith had lashed her astonished mare into a gallop and was out of the gate with Miss Cartwright's black thundering at her heels, Chilcot making a close third.

They came upon Rodney in a very few minutes and while the two ladies endeavoured to staunch the flow of blood from his wound, Chilcot was despatched back to the house to fetch aid and have Dr Merriman summoned.

'This is a gunshot wound,' stated Miss Cartwright whose Peninsula experience had put her in the way of recognizing such things. 'And an excessively gory one, 'pon my word. Thank Heaven you are not so milky as to go off into a swoon at the sight of blood, Judith.'

Miss Hammerton paid her no heed. She had pillowed the Viscount's head in her lap and was removing his neckcloth and easing his shirt-band. 'Are your neighbours in the habit of putting a bullet through any stranger who rides over their lands?' went on Miss Cartwright casually, delving under her skirts to rip off the deep flounce from her cambric petticoat. 'There, that should be adequate for the purpose. Now, let us have this coat off.'

'I cannot conceive what should have happened!' burst out Judith in an anguished way as she assisted her friend to bind up the wound securely and fashion a rough sling to hold the injured arm against the Viscount's chest. At that moment Rodney opened his eyes and the first thing his gaze fell upon was Miss Cartwright's intent face.

'Good God, Georgy, where have you come from?' he asked in a mildly surprised manner.

'Lisbon,' she returned briefly. 'Can you sit up a trifle while we pass this sling around your neck?' But Rodney was looking at Judith in the most bemused way.

'I thought you the most beautiful creature I had ever seen,' he muttered thickly. 'I — still — do.' His head dropped back and his eyes closed.

'Gone off again,' pronounced Miss Cartwright, her keen glance not missing anything of Judith's confusion at the Viscount's utterance.

'His lordship is — is wandering a trifle. He mistakes me for some other,' said Judith hurriedly.

Miss Cartwright looked her disbelief but was unable to voice it because Chilcot and a couple of stout farmhands were approaching with a door which they had taken off its hinges and upon which they proceeded to lay the Viscount, wrapped closely in a horse blanket which the groom had also thought to provide.

As they made their way with care down to the Old Hall, the two ladies following behind, leading their horses, Miss Cartwright laid a hand on Judith's arm.

'Until we can discover from his own lips what precisely took place,' she murmured, 'can these good fellows be trusted to hold their tongues?'

'Just what I had in mind,' replied Miss Hammerton, equally low, 'but why you should —'

'Something your father said to me about fearing that Quendon's path might not be entirely smooth when he came to claim his inheritance.'

'I understood you to have met my father only by chance at Lisbon,' countered Judith shrewdly. 'Yet you appear to have discussed — a number of things in detail.'

Miss Cartwright, despite a slightly heightened colour, made no reply, and, as they entered the yard, Judith, her mind a prey to the most horrid suspicions and doubts, turned her attention to seeing Rodney's insensible form safely disposed in the bedchamber that had been hurriedly prepared for his reception.

After that there were Dr Merriman's attentions to be endured, and the Viscount's only clear impressions were uncommonly painful ones, from which he was mercifully released by a generous dose of laudanum.

When he awakened from his drugged sleep he could not at first recollect where he was or how he had got there, but concluded it must be early morning by the quiet all about him and the faint glimmer of grey showing at the edge of the window drapes. As his eyes grew accustomed to the half-light, he found himself to be in a spacious bedroom which bore no resemblance whatever to the gloomy chamber he had occupied at Netherdene. The warming flames of a considerable fire reflected off polished wood and silver dressing-table appointments and, as he turned his head to inspect his surroundings in more detail, a dainty French clock on the mantelshelf struck five silvery notes. Immediately, as if by summons, the door opened to admit a tall lean figure which he had no difficulty in recognizing as his valet.

'What the devil are you doing here?'

Weak though was his master's voice, the shock of hearing it was almost sufficient to cause Parsons to drop the skep of kindling he was carrying.

'I had not imagined — how is it with you, my lord?'

'Thought I'd stuck my spoon in the wall, did you? No such thing — though I confess I'm as feeble as a kitten.'

'Indeed, my lord, and it is no great wonder,' said Parsons earnestly, setting down his load. 'The young lady informed me you have suffered a severe wound and your new riding-coat is ruined, quite ruined!'

To judge of the valet's injured tones he considered the latter of these misfortunes to be more worthy of lamentation than the former, but Rodney, overcome by drowsiness, only murmured: 'Don't bother me now, there's a good fellow,' and went to sleep again before his indignant henchman could elaborate upon the sad theme of the damage sustained by Schweitzer and Davidson's elegant creation.

When Rodney awoke again the morning was well advanced and the room bright with sunshine. At first he lay unmoving, conscious only of a great sense of lassitude and a dull ache in his injured arm. Then he observed a bowl of spring flowers on the table beside his bed and hesitantly put out a hand to touch their fresh petals. The movement, slight as it was, attracted immediate attention, for there was a soft rustle of skirts and, at once, Miss Hammerton was at his side.

'Drink a little of this, my lord.' Obediently he swallowed from the glass she held to his lips. 'You have woken most opportunely, for Dr Merriman has this moment entered the house.' As she spoke the doctor's voice could be heard in conversation with Miss Routledge as they ascended the stairs. Judith set down the glass and glanced out of the window. 'And here, if I mistake not, comes Lord Penston and — yes, Mr Edgecombe with him, to enquire how you go on.'

'Miss Hammerton,' he said diffidently, 'it is not seemly that I should be a charge on your kindness —' but she only smiled and shook her head at him as the door opened to admit Miss Routledge and Dr Merriman.

'Now let us see how my second patient fares — in fact, my only patient, for I must tell you, ma'am, that Miss Routledge has discharged herself from my care, declaring herself to be in prime twig!' pronounced the doctor.

'Which I take leave to doubt,' said Judith, 'but there is no talking to her when she takes a fit of the stubborns!'

'I should think not, indeed!' retorted Miss Routledge, advancing to the bedside. 'How are you this morning, my lord?'

'Tolerably comfortable, I thank you, ma'am, and doubtless will remain so if our good doctor will but leave me in peace.'

'That, my lord, I may not do for I must renew the dressing of the wound and be assured it has not taken on any angry humour.'

'I perceive Lord Penston and Mr Edgecombe have called,' Judith put in swiftly. 'Could you, of your kindness, receive them, Miss Patience? I can lend the doctor what assistance he needs.'

Rodney, resolved to put a brave face on it, yet could not refrain from wincing as the doctor probed and dressed his arm. At once his other hand, lying clenched on the coverlet, was clasped tightly in both of Judith's. Looking up at her gratefully, he was much moved by the depth of compassion apparent in her eyes and fancied that he perceived some other emotion there too — hopefully a partiality for her patient not altogether engendered by his unhappy state.

Dr Merriman did his business deftly and in silence, nodding his head in a satisfied way when he had finished.

'You'll do very well, my lord,' he claimed. 'As clean a wound as ever I saw. How did it come about? Some shicer out with a gun he could not handle?'

'So I believe and, had my horse not stumbled, it could have been the death of me.'

'Thank God then it was no worse. No more talking now, my lord,' said the doctor, then, turning to Judith, went on, 'a little gruel, perhaps, and as much sleep and rest as possible. I will call again this evening. Meantime — ah, good-morning, my lord.' This last remark was addressed to Lord Penston who had entered the room, wearing an air of deep concern.

'How do you find him, Doctor?'

As well as can be hoped for — do not, I beg of you, wear him down with talking. The loss of so much blood has left him very weak but, being a young man of strong constitution, that will soon put itself right. Good-morning, Mr Edgecombe. Just a few minutes only, gentlemen.'

As Judith ushered the doctor out, Mr Edgecombe stood discreetly aside while Lord Penston held low-voiced conversation with Rodney. 'What in God's name befell you, lad? Some trigger-light poacher?'

'I must suppose so since he did not offer to show himself, though he must have been aware of what he had done. A man innocent of any offence other than carelessness must surely have come to my aid, for I called out.'

'One might be forgiven for thinking so. Thank Heaven you took no greater hurt.'

'I well might have.' Rodney turned to look towards Mr Edgecombe who, one hand resting negligently upon the panelled wall, appeared to be giving a somewhat indifferent flower painting more close attention than its execution deserved. 'I have your horse to thank for that, cousin. Had he not fallen foul of a tree-root you could be calling yourself Lord Quendon to-day.'

'Now for this do I reward him with the most tasty of nosebags or give him a proper box-Harry?'

Mr Edgecombe's tone was light but his eyes were guarded. Rodney smiled. 'He's a prime fast 'un, Edgecombe, took the Long Stretch in his stride.'

'I thought that would tempt you.' Mr Edgecombe, hands thrust deep into his breeches pockets, was very much at his ease. 'How did you find the roof at Eltham?'

'Quite incomprehensible!' admitted Rodney. 'What, if you please, is bomanteek?'

Mr Edgecombe grinned. 'As I understand it, a substance for stopping up cracks in wood, but ask Sowerby, your agent, he's a local man. I am about to take my leave of you, if that suits your convenience, Quendon. I don't care to be leaving my aunt alone for too long, though she protests she does very well without me. Would you wish me to leave Trumpeter for your use?'

'I doubt I'll be riding inside of a se'ennight, but thank you for your courtesy.'

'I'll be your coachey,' volunteered Penston, 'when you feel stout enough to leave your bed.'

'Then I'll be away.' Mr Edgecombe held out his hand. 'A speedy recovery to full health, my lord. I will ride over to see how you go on in a few days' time.'

'My thanks, Edgecombe.'

When the door had closed behind him, Lord Penston said thoughtfully: 'What time of day was it precisely when you suffered this — ah, mishap?'

'Time?' Rodney frowned in thought. 'I believe — yes, I left Chedwell at four o'clock. Perhaps half an hour later? I cannot be more exact. Why do you ask?'

'Edgecombe took a gun out about three o'clock and came back around five with a few rabbits.'

Rodney stared at him. 'You cannot be suggesting —'

'I am not suggesting anything — yet, but there is something out of true here.'

'If,' said Rodney slowly, 'anyone was bent on my destruction there was ample opportunity for a second shot, for I was dazed and attempting to steady my horse.'

'Ah, but then it would not have appeared to be a shot fired by mischance. A second shot would have declared intent should anyone have been within earshot or you survive to tell the tale.'

'You would think him capable of that? I cannot accept it, sir.'

'Whatever's the truth of it, he's not best pleased to find you snugly tucked up in Miss Hammerton's guest bedroom!' said Penston significantly. 'He seems much at home at the Old Hall.'

'And Trumpeter chose the way here rather than to Netherdene,' mused Rodney.

'A source of great irritation to her ladyship, I may say! I left her lamenting the necessity for having to make a call here by reason of your being so ill-advised as to prefer the Old Hall as a sanctuary to Netherdene! And that,' he said, noting the look of strain on his godson's face, 'is enough of prosing — and here comes yet another devoted attendant,' he added as the door opened to admit Miss Cartwright bearing a bowl of gruel.

'Georgy!' exclaimed the Viscount, 'then I did not dream you?'

'Certainly you did not,' she returned coolly. 'And if you will be so obliging as to swallow this nauseous concoction, I will tell you briefly how my presence here comes about.' She then persuaded the Viscount to partake of the gruel and informed him of her more recent adventures.

'So you have seen Mr Hammerton?' he asked in surprise.

'Yes, and you will shortly have that pleasure yourself,' she assured him. 'In the meantime, he asked me to convey a message to you, should we meet, to step warily.'

'What can he mean by that?'

'I cannot say but, to judge of to-day's incident, it is not inapt advice.'

'Do not tell me that you, too, subscribe to the belief that I was shot by ill-intent?'

'Poachers are not usually so careless of their firearms,' she pointed out.

'Well, then, let us allow it to have been some fellow after rabbits or pigeon,' said Rodney a little impatiently, 'who, finding no sport, goes a bit on the fret and looses off at anything that moves.'

She pursed her lips. 'Maybe,' was all she would say. Lord Penston was watching her closely.

'But you think otherwise, Miss Cartwright?' he asked quietly.

'Let us say I have been put on the alert by Mr Hammerton's warning. He is not a fanciful man nor one to see danger where none exists.' So saying, she removed Rodney's empty bowl. 'Now, I will send your valet to you and then you must rest.'

Rodney lay, a prey to puzzled speculation, until Parsons came to shave and divert him with items of local interest gleaned from kitchen and stableyard. His master took small heed of the valet's gossiping tongue until he remarked:

'Mr Edgecombe's left us, my lord, and cook's in a rare taking for she had prepared him a dish of Pegwell Bay shrimps such as he likes, and he'd not stay to eat them.'

'She knows his tastes, then?'

'Oh, he's a regular caller here, I'm given to understand,' said Parsons with the air of one who holds himself to be above such finicking items of news. 'Very taken with the young lady, I'm told, and who's to wonder at it?' He darted an inquisitive glance from under his eyelids to see how his lordship was taking this interesting intelligence, but the Viscount merely murmured: 'Who, indeed?' which caused Parsons to feel some concern for his master's health since he was never one to be behind the fair in paying his addresses to beautiful young women.

Dr Merriman professed himself to be well satisfied with his patient's condition when he called again towards the evening. Rodney, who had spent the day drifting in and out of sleep, was feeling greatly refreshed and was insistent that there was no call for a constant watch to be kept over him during the night. Thus it was that, when he awoke at some time in the dark hours, he was not surprised to find himself alone and lay, quiescent, for a time, watching the firelight casting long shadows across the floor. A slight creaking sound drew his attention and then a stealthy movement. Now fully conscious, he was aware that someone had entered his room and was approaching the bed. Presuming this to be Parsons satisfying himself that all was well, he turned his head on the pillow to look towards the door, then made the disconcerting discovery that the sound of movement came from quite another direction. His first thought was that someone had climbed in at a window, but it was a fresh blustery night and no breath of wind disturbed the still warmth of the room. Yet he was tolerably certain that he was not alone and was about to challenge the intruder when the door-latch lifted with a soft click to admit Miss Cartwright, bearing a branch of candles.

Instantly, though no sound of footfall could be heard on the thick carpet, there was a rustle and again that faint creaking noise coming from the shadowed corner of the room. Miss Cartwright stood for a moment, staring in that direction, then she stepped briskly forward.

'Awake, Quendon? Are you not comfortable?'

'Comfortable enough in body,' he answered her. 'But — I think I am starting at shadows, Georgy.'

'Now don't be telling me you've seen a ghost!' she implored him, setting down her candles. 'For I'll not believe you.'

'If I saw anything, which is not at all certain,' said Rodney, closing his eyes as if to sleep again. Then he opened them suddenly. 'What are you about at this hour? I thought it was agreed that no night watch was to be kept over me?'

She smiled and settled herself in a chair. 'Parsons has been with you until now but I have dismissed him to his bed, for he has been on his feet for close on twenty-four hours, and William, the footman, will take my place at midnight.'

'You are not sitting here until midnight!' he protested.

'Oh, yes, I am,' she informed him. 'So you had best go to sleep again.'

'My dear Georgy, it is hardly proper!'

She glanced at the clock. 'There is little more than half an hour to go and, in any case, you are in no condition to be other than proper!' she pointed out.

He was forced to agree with her on that head, so closed his eyes again. Miss Cartwright, once assured he was asleep, lit another branch of candles and placed them in the furthest corner of the room where they appeared to serve no purpose other than to throw light upon that same flower painting that Mr Edgecombe had found so worthy of his interest earlier in the day. Then she turned her chair so as to face in that direction and, opening up the book she had brought with her, prepared to while away the time by acquainting herself with the writings of Mr George Crabbe.

CHAPTER
SEVEN

THE dowager was in no conciliatory humour. In her considered opinion, Quendon had displayed a lack of good sense in being shot at in the Home Wood, she was quite out of charity with him; while for him to be recuperating from his wound at the Old Hall was the outside of enough.

'A most dubious establishment,' she animadverted to her daughter, 'supported by money made in trade.'

'I understand Miss Routledge to be a very superior sort of woman,' Euphrasia ventured to suggest. 'A cousin of my lord Yeovil.'

Lady Quendon declined to be impressed by any such connection. 'Most great men have their hangers-on,' she proclaimed largely, 'and every family its impecunious relatives. No, I consider Quendon to have shown a remarkable want of purpose in failing to guide his horse back to Netherdene.'

'But, mama, Dr Merriman declares Quendon to be gravely hurt.'

'Pooh!' The dowager dismissed Dr Merriman and his pretensions with a wave of the hand. 'A country doctor with too great an opinion of himself. It is to his advantage, I dare say, to pretend that his lordship's hurt is of a serious nature so that he may reap the greater credit for his recovery. I do not recall having heard that Quendon is of a sickly disposition; such an injury must be of small account to a healthy young man.'

Euphrasia said no more but, being the possessor of more commonsense than her parent gave her credit for, she was deeply troubled. Mr Jasper Edgecombe's careless kindness to his shy little cousin had quite won her heart and, of latter years, that childish adoration had changed to a more durable emotion. He had said very little to her on the score of the new Viscount, but then he did not have to, for she guessed at his feelings all too well. Yet, she argued, he could never have hoped to succeed when her two stepbrothers and, after them, Sir Rollo Nairn and his son stood between him and the title. Who could have foreseen that these four obstacles would be reduced so dramatically to one in so few years? With only a single life between him and his ambition did Jasper feel impelled to give Fate a nudge?

She shivered suddenly and her mother kindly advised her to go and fetch a shawl to put round her shoulders. But it was not Netherdene's whistling draughts that had chilled Euphrasia, it was the memory of Mr Edgecombe boasting lightly that he could get in and out of the Old Hall at will, without ever anyone knowing he had set foot in the place. The existence of a secret passage was common knowledge, for her father had informed Mr Hammerton of it when he had bought the house, and she understood it to have been made secure, so Jasper must have knowledge of some other entrance. Again she shivered, and this time the dowager's recommendation was peremptory.

With a muttered apology, she rose and hurried from the room — not, as might be supposed, upstairs for her shawl, but to the book-room where, to her surprise, she found Lord Penston. He smiled at her pleasantly as she stood, hesitant, in the doorway.

'Forgive me, Miss Edgecombe, if I intrude. I confess it to be simple curiosity that brings me here.'

Euphrasia liked his lordship. He was kind and courteous, and always gave her the comfortable feeling that she was a person in whose company he took pleasure which, to one more accustomed to scolds and set-downs than compliments, was a matter for some gratification. She assured him that he was in no way intruding and asked if he had news of Quendon's condition.

'Yes, I have but returned from the Old Hall. He passed a reasonably easy night and Merriman says the wound is healing as cleanly as could be wished for. Quendon talks of returning to Netherdene as soon as he may so as to relieve the ladies at the Old Hall of the burden of caring for him, so I have no doubt we shall see him here in a day or two when I can take him in charge.'

'Oh, I must inform mama,' said Euphrasia impulsively, 'for if he is coming back so soon she will have no need to call —' She stopped and blushed most becomingly.

Penston, thinking that, if she had the first notion of how to dress and was removed from her mother's oppressive influence, she could be quite a taking little thing, could not resist murmuring: 'Fortunate, is it not?' with such a marked twinkle in his eye that her confusion was turned to amusement.

'Yes, well, you know mama! She feels that Quendon showed a great lack of consideration in not directing his horse back to Netherdene!'

'Very understandable!' nodded his lordship. 'But I am of the opinion that Quendon's thoughts were less bent on regard for her ladyship's sensibilities than on clinging fast to the saddle and praying that Trumpeter would see him safe! Which, to be sure, he did.'

'Yes, to the Old Hall,' she said doubtfully.

'A most interesting building, is it not?' he said in his easy way. 'Miss Hammerton has told me something of its history. It belonged to your family, I am given to understand, until Mr Hammerton bought it from your father.'

'Oh, yes,' she said, eager to discuss a subject on which she was well informed. 'It was used to be a very much larger house, you know, parts of it go back to the fifteenth century, but some ancestor of ours found himself put to the pinch and pulled down a wing. The cellars, however, remain and extend over a vast area outside the confines of the present house.'

'Indeed?' His lordship displayed a gratifying interest. 'Is there, by chance, a plan that shows the whole of the original building? Miss Hammerton tells me there is none such in her possession.'

'Yes, I am sure there is.' Miss Edgecombe, who had come in search of that very thing herself, moved over to one of the bookcases and, pulling out a number of volumes, revealed a small cupboard set in the wall behind them. 'In fact, I *know* there is because my cousin Jasper showed me one a long time ago. In latter years the Old Hall was occupied by his parents, you see, and he spent his boyhood there — oh, until he was past twenty, when his father died and he and his mother removed to Thaxted.'

'So he knows the house very well?'

'Indeed, yes,' said she, bringing out a roll of parchments and laying them on the table. 'It must have been a fascinating home for a boy — all hidden nooks and crannies and even a secret passage.'

She pulled herself up sharply and cast a doubtful glance at Penston, but he was idly swinging his quizzing-glass and looking no more than politely diverted. Reassured, Euphrasia turned her attention to sorting through the documents. She would have been less easy in her mind had she known of the trenchant conversation he had held not an hour before with Miss Cartwright on the subject of nocturnal visitors.

'I thought it to have been a trick of the light,' Georgiana had told him, 'a shadow fantasy, for I was still not seeing clearly beyond the scope of the candles when I entered the room, but Quendon knew there had been someone there for all he tried to pass it off as an over-feverish imagination. But I'll swear he was not feverish. In my opinion the sooner he is out of this house the better.'

'I will have him away the moment Merriman gives his approval,' Penston had promised, and, as he looked over Euphrasia's shoulder to study the yellowing document spread upon the table, he vowed to put this intention into effect without delay. Before him lay the full plan of the Old Hall, with the portion that had been pulled down indicated by dotted lines. The secret passage was clearly marked and a thinly traced line seemed to indicate the presence of another passage leading off it to the upstairs landing and at least one bedroom — that in which Rodney was at present lodged.

'How interesting!' he remarked, assisting the lady to hold the parchment flat upon the table.

'Y-yes, m-most!' she said, rather breathlessly, for she, too, had comprehended the significance of that faint line. 'But there should be an older map than this, the original plan for the house. I cannot but feel that it must be in Mr Hammerton's possession.'

'No doubt, but it is of no great matter after all,' he assured her kindly. She looked at him in a piteous way and he shrewdly guessed at what she was thinking. 'Perhaps Mr Edgecombe may have knowledge of its whereabouts?' he suggested, rolling up the

TAKE THESE 3 free Masquerade HISTORICALS

That's right! THREE first-rate MASQUERADE HISTORICAL romance novels by world renowned authors, FREE, as your introduction to the MASQUERADE HISTORICAL Subscription Plan.

Your FREE Gift Includes

A Rose for Danger
by Marguerite Bell.

18th Century England. No man had ever stirred Juliet's emotions like the handsome Sir Nicholas Childe. But dare she become involved? Was he an infamous highwayman — or the answer to her dreams?

Francesca
by Valentina Luellen.

In Renaissance Italy, amid palace intrigue, Francesca finds herself caught in the struggle between her husband and her brother. Can she save them both? Can she save herself?

Madelon
by Valentina Luellen.

11th Century Spain. Beautiful but innocent Madelon is saved from slavery by her brother's mortal enemy, the dashing Valentin — and forced to choose between family loyalty . . . and passion.

Relive, through the pages of these exciting novels, the endless ages, the timeless vistas of romance.

Explore with MASQUERADE HISTORICALS, the times of antiquity, the Middle Ages, the Rennaisance, the Regency and Victorian eras . . . all the epoch making centuries, a whole new adventure with MASQUERADE HISTORICALS. Capture, on each page, the taste and texture of those bygone eras, the action, romance, adventure and intrigue.

plan with the other documents and replacing them in the cupboard.

'No, no, I am perfectly certain he has not!' she said, rather too quickly, and he felt a start of sympathy for her, so anxious as she was that Jasper should not be involved and so fearful that he might be. Yet he was deeply uneasy in his mind at the thought of Rodney lying helpless at the Old Hall unaware of any malignant influence threatening his safety.

In this assumption he proved to be mistaken, for Judith's quick understanding had comprehended that something was amiss. Georgiana's questions about secret passages and her insistence on having someone in constant attendance in the Viscount's room would have alerted a much less keen intelligence. Idly she enquired of Miss Routledge if she had any knowledge of a house plan prior to the pulling-down of the old wing.

Miss Routledge set a few more stitches to her embroidery, then adjusted the Argand brass lamp on the table at her side.

'I believe we are running low in spermacetti oil,' she remarked. 'I must instruct Chilcot to obtain some to-morrow when he goes to Saffron Walden.' Judith said nothing but waited until Miss Routledge went on with some reluctance. 'I believe there is such a plan amongst the papers your father left with me to be kept close until his return. Why do you wish to see it?'

'Because,' said Judith tranquilly, 'I have reason to think that some use is being made of the old cellars at the present time which may disturb our — peace of mind.'

Miss Routledge looked as if she was about to ask for further enlightenment but, changing her mind, set aside her tambour and rose.

'I must go to release Parsons now,' she said. 'Lord Penston spoke of returning after dinner to stand duty from eight o'clock until midnight.'

Judith shut her book with a decisive snap and went to look out of the window. 'It is time and enough that Georgy was returned from Bishop's Stortford. The sky is heavy with rain.'

Her words fell upon the empty air for Miss Routledge had left the room and, with a shrug of surprise, Judith seated herself by the window to take advantage of what light there was, and continued her reading. Presently Miss Routledge returned and handed her a document, wrapped in silk.

'Handle it with care,' she entreated. 'It is, your father believes, the plan of the building made when it was enlarged in 1625. Place it in my drawer of the desk when you have perused it.'

'Thank you, Miss Patience.'

Left alone, Judith unrolled the parchment and, in a moment, had found what she was seeking. 'But how can this be?' she murmured, half-aloud. 'If the main passage has been blocked — and that, I know was done — how can the other which leads off it be used?' A few seconds' thought gave her the answer. 'By entering from one of the house entrances, of course! But they were secured, too, of that I am certain.'

Swiftly wrapping the plan up once more in its silk covering, she bestowed it in Miss Routledge's drawer of the double-sided writing-table. Then, going into the outer hall, she stood listening for a moment. A few distant sounds came from the kitchen quarters, but at four o'clock in the afternoon most of the staff were still taking their ease. Mounting upon an oak settle, she took down a heavily-framed painting of a peaceful rural scene which she had caused to be hung there because, privately, she considered it to be a little dull, though her father claimed that any work of John Constable's would be eagerly sought after in years to come and, setting it carefully against the wall, she pressed and pushed at the panelling behind and around where it had hung. Eventually, her fingers found the catch. They also found the nail that had been driven in to prevent its being moved. Satisfied that no one had used that mode of entry, she replaced the painting and climbed down.

'To the dining-room next,' she decided. 'Else Jessop will be coming to set the covers for dinner and will find me climbing about the wall!' Giggling a little at the very notion of her butler's shocked amazement, she entered the silent, rather gloomy room and sniffed in disapproval at the lingering odour of the previous night's meal that still hung on the air. 'I'll vow no one has been in to freshen the place to-day,' she sighed, flinging open a window and being rewarded by a strong gust of wind that stirred the hangings and dispelled the heavy atmosphere. When alone, she and Miss Routledge took their meals in the breakfast parlour and, doubtless, Jessop hoped that this comfortable practice would establish itself again after the first few days of Miss Cartwright's stay. 'Well, it won't and so he shall discover!' declared his mistress crossly. 'Now, where is this panel?'

As she could not clearly remember where the catch was concealed, it took her a greater to time to discover than she had anticipated, and when she did it was as firmly secured as the one in the hall had been. She had just got down from her chair and was setting it back at the table when the door opened and Jessop appeared, bearing an armful of freshly-laundered table-linen. The breeze, striking between open door and window, promptly lifted the topmost napkins off the pile and scattered them about the room like so many broken-winged doves while one, more imaginative than the rest, settled upon the astonished butler's head, looking like nothing so much as a dunce's cap.

Striving to preserve her gravity in face of Jessop's patent disapproval, she delivered a stricture on the ill-kept condition of the room, advised him to see to it without delay, and swept out, almost knocking down a small maidservant, armed with brushes and dusters, whose function was plainly to set the room to rights. Then the sound of Miss Cartwright's voice resigned her to abandoning her investigation and drew her back to the hall.

'Georgy! What a time you have been! Were things to your liking?'

'Nothing could be better!' declared Miss Cartwright, pulling off her bonnet and shaking the raindrops from her burnished locks. 'Fairacre is perfectly habitable and has been excellently tended by the couple my father put to live there. They have but to strip off the Holland covers and light a few fires and I and my Accoutrements can move in to-morrow.'

'Oh, not to-morrow!' protested Judith. 'We had hoped to have you with us for at least a se'ennight.'

To be truthful, I told them by the end of next week, for I would wish the wagon to go over first and I must see to its unloading. But it was a most pleasing surprise to find everything in such capital order.' She put an arm around Judith's waist and led her into the book-room. 'And how have you been occupying yourself in my absence? No more incidents or excitements to recount?'

Light though her tone might be, there was that in her regard that gave Judith cause to wonder if her friend did indeed expect to hear of further unprecedented happenings. For some reason that she could not quite justify to herself, she decided to keep her own counsel on the matter of the secret passage, and so answered in an equally casual manner.

'No, nothing worthy of mention. Quendon goes on famously, talks of leaving us as soon as Dr Merriman permits.'

'Oh-ho! Has a fancy to be ministered to by her ladyship and Miss Euphrasia, has he? Ungrateful creatures, gentlemen, are they not?'

Miss Cartwright then embarked on an animated account of her excursion to Bishop's Stortford until interrupted by Jessop, who came to announce that a Mrs Woolcott had called.

'I have ushered her into the saloon, miss,' he said, his tone expressing strong disapprobation of persons who paid social calls at an hour when the staff might be supposed to be fully occupied with the preparation of dinner which, in accordance with country hours, was taken at the Old Hall at six o'clock.

'Thank you, Jessop. Please inform her that I shall not keep her waiting above a moment or two. Now why,' she added when he had withdrawn, 'should Mrs Woolcott be so condescending as to pay me a call? Hitherto it has not suited her consequence to acknowledge my existence.'

'A friend of the dowager's?' hazarded Georgiana.

'They are as close as ames-ace,' admitted Judith.

'Then, depend upon it, she has learned of Quendon's mishap and has come to inform herself more minutely of all the circumstances. You'd best attend her, Judith, while I change out of these dusty garments.'

'Join me when you can or set Miss Patience free to do so. I believe her to be sitting with Quendon.'

So saying, Judith went to greet her visitor. Mrs Woolcott was short in stature and possessed of a full habit of body which was in no wise diminished by her mode of dress. This was distinguished by more frills and flounces, ribbons and trinkets, than Judith could ever remember seeing on any one person at the same time. Beneath her deep-brimmed bonnet the frilled edge of a cornette framed a round, pink countenance that might have earned the epithet of 'cherubic' had not the sharp glint of a pair of very knowing eyes and the downward droop of a tightly-pursed mouth belied any such kindly adjective.

She was, however, all affable condescension, and apologized for the late hour of her call which she explained very readily by saying she had been taking tea with Lady Quendon, who had informed her of the Viscount's unhappy accident.

'And you must know, Miss Hammerton, as I was the bearer of an invitation to the Netherdene household to dine with me when it should suit their convenience, I at once conceived the notion of asking you and your friend, Miss Cartwright, to be of the party. Sir Humphrey Cartwright's daughter, is she not? Such an amiable gentleman, I am given to understand, and quite a bosom friend of the late Lord Quendon.'

If this intelligence was something of a revelation to Judith, she gave no sign of it but, seating herself beside the lady, said everything that was right and proper, so that her visitor was disposed to think that Lady Quendon had mistaken the matter when she claimed the household at the Old Hall to be nothing above the ordinary. A suitable date was agreed upon to dine at Woolcott Manor though, of course, as Judith made clear, she could not answer for the Viscount as she was in full expectation of his being back at Netherdene in a few days.

'So unfortunate an occurrence! And on his lordship's very first visit here!' It might be inferred from Mrs Woolcott's shocked tones that had the incident taken place on Rodney's second or third visit to Netherdene then it could be regarded in a more lenient light. 'He will have no great opinion of us, I dare say. Geoffrey — that is my eldest son, you know — is quite in a puzzle as to how it should have come about.'

At that moment, to Judith's relief, they were joined by Miss Cartwright, impeccably gowned in pale-pink cambric over a petticoat of white satin, with a handsome Lyons shawl of flowered silk draped over her shoulders.

Judith, marvelling at her friend's rapid change of dress, presented her to Mrs Woolcott and thereafter was relieved of all participation in the conversation since Miss Cartwright bore her share of the platitudes and compliments bestowed upon her with commendable fortitude, responding to them in so sweetly deprecating a manner that Judith, who well knew Georgiana's dislike of toad-eaters, was hard put to it to keep her countenance.

When, at last, Mrs Woolcott took her departure, still protesting that she must surely be the envy of all to number two such taking young ladies among her dinner guests, Miss Cartwright fixed Miss Hammerton with a very cold eye.

'I think it most ill-done of you, my hostess,' she said in a distinctly contumelious manner, 'to burden us with such an engagement. It would serve you well if I took myself off to Fairacre and left you to face the ordeal alone!'

'Oh, Georgy, you would not be so callous!' protested Judith. 'Could you but have seen your face when she was enthusing over *dear* Sir Humphrey!'

'I'd best be sure of cutting *that* connection before he returns home, else he'll not thank me for it! She is just the sort of female he can least abide, an addle-pated gossip who aspires to a consequence which rests solely on a foundation compounded of the number of titled or well-bred persons to whom she may make her bow.'

'As I answer in neither respect I must presume that the combined dignity of Sir Humphrey and Lord Yeovil outweigh my inferior standing,' sighed Judith in mock humility. 'Great Heaven! I must go at once to change my dress else I shall be in Miss Patience's bad books!'

'And I must write a note to be carried over to Fairacre the first thing to-morrow morning, with instructions for the disposition of some furniture in order to make space for what is in the wagon — quite feather-witted of me to have forgot to arrange for it this afternoon. May I use your writing-table?'

'Yes, of course. It is Miss Patience's also for, being double-sided, we both make free of it. You will find writing-paper and wafers there to hand. Forgive me, I must go.'

It was not until she was in her bedchamber and her maid was

unbuttoning her gown that she remembered she had placed the plan of the Old Hall in the desk where Georgiana could scarcely fail to see it did she use Miss Routledge's drawer, but a moment's reflection assured her that this could hardly signify since Miss Cartwright was as alert as anyone to the danger that might threaten the Viscount. Nonetheless, she wished with all her heart that her father would soon return to take over the care of his household.

CHAPTER EIGHT

MISS HAMMERTON was not the only inmate of the Old Hall to wish for the return of the master of the house. Miss Routledge, although she had not been taken into anyone's confidence on the subject of their guest's safety, yet could not but be sensible of the atmosphere of unrest that pervaded the establishment, while Miss Cartwright who, by reason of her Peninsular experiences, had been granted undisputed command of the sickroom was most uneasy in her mind.

Rodney himself, though a sensitive and alert young gentleman enough, was not given to over-imaginative flights of fancy, and was disposed to take a commonsense view of the whole affair. The shooting in the Home Wood most likely was an accident; the fact that Trumpeter had led him to the Old Hall rather than to Netherdene was, doubtless, purely coincidental; but when one added to these two imponderables the visitation of the previous night then any sensible man might be pardoned for wondering if there should not be a regular purpose behind these disturbing incidents.

The possibility that his cousin Jasper was the *deus ex machina* behind the sequence of events did not readily commend itself to him. In his opinion, Jasper was too obvious a culprit and by far too shrewd a man to place himself under suspicion had he the intention of causing hurt to Rodney. Yet the facts were indisputable. He had directed the Viscount's homeward path from Chedwell Farm in so skilful a manner as almost to ensure his taking the way through the Home Wood; he had lent him Trumpeter to ride, and that sagacious animal was clearly well-used to approaching the Old Hall from that direction; he could well have primed the farmer and his wife at Chedwell to see that their guest did not return through the lanes, but at this point

Rodney called a halt to his deliberations. The thought of his kindly host and hostess mixing such treachery with their hospitality was carrying suspicion too far.

What, then, was the answer? For no reason that he could precisely define, he did not wish to think ill of Mr Edgecombe. This he endeavoured to explain to his godfather when that astute gentleman came, as he expressed it, to do his spell of guard duty that evening, but Lord Penston was not of the same mind.

'It is the likeness to your father that makes you feel you owe some loyalty to Edgecombe.'

'But I cannot believe —'

'No matter what you believe, I intend to prevail upon Merriman to allow you to be moved to Netherdene to-morrow. Now, go to sleep, there's a good fellow. I have a rattling fine novel here of Walter Scott's, so give me leave to enjoy it.'

This, the Viscount obediently did, and Penston immersed himself in the adventures of *Guy Mannering* until certain sounds that seemed to him to be rather more significant than the old house's acceptable creaks caused him to raise his head and listen intently. He glanced at the clock which showed close on midnight and time that he aroused Parsons. Carefully placing a marker in his book, he rose and went to look at Rodney as he slept, cheek pillowed on hand, dark hair engagingly disarrayed, and a faint smile curving his lips. Penston mused again on how unbelievably like to his mother the young man was, and the memory of Mary Nairn gave his thoughts a turn in another direction. As if in response to these reflections, a light tap sounded on the door and Miss Routledge peeped in.

'Ma'am, I believed you to be in your bed a good hour past!'

'I have been writing long overdue letters,' she explained in her soft voice, 'and thought to ask Jessop to leave ready a small collation so that you may be heartened for your journey back to Netherdene.'

'Exceeding kind of you, ma'am,' he said, then, raising his voice a little, continued, 'I was just about to rout out Parsons from his bed. Quendon is sleeping soundly so I think we may safely leave him.' So saying, he followed her out of the room.

closing the door with what she considered to be unnecessary firmness, though she failed to observe that he pushed it slightly as it swung to, thereby ensuring that the latch did not fall into place, and walked along the landing with her, talking easily in a normal tone of voice. At the head of the stairs, to her astonishment, he caught her arm and murmured: 'Continue talking as you go downstairs as if I am with you.'

'Should I not arouse Parsons?' she whispered, watching in wide-eyed amazement as he removed his boots.

'Not unless I call to you. Await me below, if you will, ma'am.' He smiled at her air of bewilderment. 'Do not be in a worry, Miss Routledge. I am not quite out of my wits, at least I hope that I am not!'

He then retreated back along the landing on tip-toe, holding his boots in one hand and *Guy Mannering* in the other. Miss Routledge did not need to be told her part twice, and she descended to the hall with great dignity, talking animatedly to no one in particular. As she did, she fancied she saw a flicker of light show under the book-room door but hardly gave the matter a thought so deep was her concern at Lord Penston's very odd behaviour.

He, arrived back at the bedroom, pressed his hand steadily against the unlatched door which yielded a few inches, giving him a view of the room and Rodney asleep in the big bed, but not of the corner in which his interest lay. He waited, listening. Downstairs he could just hear Miss Routledge moving about in the saloon and the occasional murmur of her voice as if still holding a conversation with another person. Then, from inside the bedroom came a slight creaking noise and Penston poised himself to thrust wide the heavy door and spring into the room.

Unfortunately, at that moment, Miss Routledge had recalled the odd circumstance of a light showing under the book-room door and, being not at all easy in her mind about Lord Penston, she came into the hall, calling back over her shoulder, as if speaking to someone in the saloon. 'Yes, it is in the book-room, I am sure. Grant me a moment and I will fetch it.'

Her voice carried with disastrous clarity to the upper floor and Penston, understanding that anyone entering Rodney's room secretly must at once comprehend that the door to the landing was ajar, flung it open and entered without further ceremony. But he was too late. The creaking noise started once again and a darker oblong of shadow swiftly merged into the surrounding gloom. As he arrived at the panel, hands outstretched to check it, it clicked softly home and he was left staring at the unbroken surface of the oak. Impatiently, he tapped and pressed on the wood, uncomfortably aware that, in all likelihood, some other person was standing motionless on the other side, not a foot from him. Then Rodney turned and muttered in his sleep and, abandoning the attempt to discover the catch, Penston retrieved his boots which he had dropped outside the door, and sat down to pull them on.

Meanwhile Miss Routledge had entered the book-room and discovered a branch of candles alight on the table. Surprised at such unwonted carelessness on Jessop's part, she picked it up and was about to leave the room when a slight draught caused the flames to flutter and die down. Then it was she perceived the aperture by the fireplace, standing invitingly open. Setting down the candles again, she approached it cautiously and peered inside. There was little to be seen but grime and cobwebs, then she glanced down and perceived amid the dust the faint imprint of footmarks. 'Oh, no!' she breathed, indignation overcoming her natural alarm, 'how could she — without speaking of her intention to me?'

Her resolution fanned by her mounting irritation, she took down a single candlestick from the mantelshelf and lit it from one of the other candles. Grasping this resolutely in her right hand, for her sprained left wrist was still incapable of much effort, she stepped through the opening. There she hesitated for a moment as to which way to turn for the passage stretched in either direction. The way she chose meandered on for some length and, when she paused to look back, the faint glow thrown by the candles in the book-room through the open panel had become alarmingly distant. Then it vanished altogether to reappear again for a few moments before being completely extinguished.

Miss Routledge told herself firmly not to give way to high hysterics. 'Whoever opened that panel has just stepped out of the passage and closed it,' she argued in a fierce whisper,' 'and like as not, it was Judith, for I am sure that if the passage was marked upon that plan, she could not have resisted the lure of inspecting it.'

The reflection that Miss Hammerton was now probably on her way upstairs to bed, having taken the candles in the book-room with her, leaving her chaperone to spend an uncomfortable night amid the dust and cobwebs was no great comfort to Miss Routledge. Then she reminded herself that if Judith had been able to move in and out of the passage at will she surely could do no less.

Her fingers closed more tightly over the heavy brass candlestick as if to draw comfort from its weighty solidity and, having satisfied herself that the course she was pursuing led well beyond the limits of the book-room and must be continuing on to dining-room and hall, she retraced her steps until she came to the panel by which she had entered. She quickly discovered the catch that operated it but, to her dismay, it was quite immovable and she was obliged to conclude that it had been secured from the other side.

'Drat the child!' she muttered, keeping up her spirits by a semblance of irritation, though her heart sank into her now excessively grimy satin slippers at the thought that, if she could discover no other exit opening off the yet unexplored portion of the passage, she must resign herself to endure until morning in the stifling, dust-laden atmosphere and in complete darkness, for there was scarce an hour's burning left in the candle.

Refusing to be cast down by so discouraging a prospect, she proceeded briskly in the opposite direction to that which she had first pursued and presently, to her infinite relief, stumbled over a small heap of bricks and rubble, piled untidily beside an irregular opening in the outer wall of the house. Here was visible a narrow stairway, set in the thickness of the wall. For the first time the possibility that it might *not* be Miss Hammerton who had entered the passage before her presented itself to her anxious mind. 'Well, whoever it may have been has now gone,' she consoled herself bravely. 'And you may press on without fear of — of an adverse encounter.'

As she struggled up the steep, narrow stair, she appreciated how awkward any encounter would be in such cramped surroundings, and sighed with relief as she stepped out upon a small landing. Immediately in front of her was a door similar to that which gave on to the book-room below. Hopefully, she felt about for the catch but nothing responded to her touch. It was at that moment she fancied she heard a sound from the foot of the stairway, as if someone had stumbled against the loose rubble in the passage. Miss Routledge decided that the time had come to be done with secrecy. Disregarding the pain inflicted upon her injured wrist, she beat as strongly as was in her power upon the door panel, calling in a somewhat frenzied way: 'Help! Help! Let me out, if you please!'

For a moment nothing happened then she heard an exclamation in a man's voice uttered, it seemed, almost in her ear. Startled, she drew back and looked down the dark well of the stair, but nothing stirred below her. In her agitation, she put out her hand to support herself against the wall and, in so doing, inadvertently released the door catch. With a faint creak, it slid open and she fell forward into Lord Penston's arms.

'My dear Miss Patience, what can you be about?' said he, removing the candlestick from her trembling grasp and setting her down in a chair.

'My lord, I believe there is someone following — oh, have a care!' she cried as he stepped into the passage.

'There is no one there now,' he assured her, returning to her side. 'Now be so good as to inform me of what has taken place. When I went downstairs and found no trace of you, I feared for your safety.'

Briefly she told him of discovering the open panel in the book-room. 'I was persuaded it was Judith who had gone exploring, you see,' she explained, 'because I had showed her the old plan of the house on which the passage was marked.'

He stood looking down on her with a curious expression on his face. 'So you at once went off in pursuit?' he said softly. 'Intrepid Miss Patience!'

'Well, I could not be sure just why you returned here so secretly unless, perhaps, you had heard her scrambling about,' she faltered, shyly aware of being addressed as 'Miss Patience' and finding the familiarity greatly to her liking.

He took out his handkerchief. 'Allow me,' he said, and deftly removed a vestige of cobweb that clung to her cheek.

'C-can we close that panel?' she asked nervously. He shook his head.

'I have no notion where the catch may be,' he confessed, turning to look at the dark aperture. Then his eye fell on the flower painting hanging near to it and his visual memory supplied the picture of Mr Jasper Edgecombe studying that painting while his hand rested negligently upon the woodwork. With a muttered imprecation, Penston placed himself in a like posture, his fingers sliding over the carved acanthus leaves that embellished the panelling until, to Miss Routledge's relieved astonishment, there was a small sound and the panel closed.

'How — how did you know to do that?' she asked.

'Shall we say guided by an inspired guess?' His lordship's expression was very grim. 'Now, ma'am, may I escort you to your room, or do you conceive it to be your duty to confront Miss Hammerton on the subject of her midnight perambulations?'

'I — I do not believe it was Judith,' she said in a small voice.

He had taken her hand in his and was scrutinizing it carefully. 'My poor dear, that wrist is very inflamed,' he remarked and kissed it. 'If not Miss Hammerton, then who was it?'

Miss Routledge, feeling that the situation was getting thoroughly out of hand and that she was behaving in not at all a sensible manner, whispered: 'I don't know, but — but I allowed myself to become foolishly frightened.'

'Frightened you may have been and with good reason, but foolish I will not allow.'

He was smiling at her so tenderly that there is no knowing what further foolishness she might not have uttered had not a gentle cough from the bed reminded them both of the presence of the Viscount, who was sitting up regarding them with some amusement.

'Oh!' she cried out in quick distress. 'I have disturbed your rest, my lord.'

'I have got the notion that my rest would have been disturbed in any case, ma'am,' he responded pleasantly. 'And possibly in a less felicitous manner. Whatever is that?'

Certain whisperings and scufflings outside the door heralded the appearance of a deputation, headed by Parsons, with the Misses Cartwright and Hammerton in close attendance. Parsons, after one horrified glance at Miss Routledge, whose dishevelled hair and dusty gown gave her all the appearance of a lady slightly demented, politely enquired of Lord Penston if he might take over his duty.

'Willingly,' came the response. 'But first, if you would be so good, please fetch me a longish nail and a hammer.'

Parsons, as well he might, looked considerably taken aback at this request and wondered where, in a strange house at that hour of night, he could lay hands on two such articles. An appealing look at Miss Hammerton evoked no help, for she was kneeling beside Miss Routledge and demanding to be told what had befallen her.

'I shall be pleased to fetch your requirements, my lord.' Jessop's voice, unexpected but urbane as ever, gave no hint of perturbation. 'May I be informed for what purpose you require the nail so that I may procure one of the proper length?'

Lord Penston walked over to the wall and operated the catch so that the panel opened once again to the accompaniment of startled gasps and exclamations from those not cognisant of its existence.

'I wish to ensure that this may not be opened by any unauthorised person,' said he briefly. 'I take it, Miss Hammerton, you can have no wish to place your guests in a room where they may be disturbed by — ah, nocturnal visitors?'

'None, sir,' she replied coolly. 'And as it is most likely that my father will occupy this room when he returns, I am even more anxious that it be made proof against any such visitations.'

Penston nodded. 'A nail of about three inches should be

sufficient,' he said to Jessop. The butler bowed and went out of the room, leaving his lordship to wonder how, amid the many hastily-arrayed persons present, Jessop should be fully dressed and, seemingly, not at all put out by so incongruous a gathering, which might reasonbly have been expected to outrage his profound sense of propriety.

Judith, having assured herself that Miss Routledge had suffered no hurt, glanced towards the bed where Miss Cartwright was talking to the Viscount. He had raised his hand to clasp one of hers and was smiling up at her in what Miss Hammerton considered to be an excessively friendly manner. The graceful tableau they presented, silhouetted against the light of the bedside candles, won no appreciation from her and she was honest enough to allow that the strong emotion which possessed her at the sight could not be described by any other name than jealousy.

Hearing her sharply indrawn breath, Miss Routledge quickly gathered her skirts together and, rising, announced that, all anxiety having now been allayed by Lord Penston's practical solution to the difficulty, she had nothing more to do than beg the pardon of all for having disturbed their rest, and counsel them to retire to their respective chambers and make what good use they could of the remaining hours of sleep left to them.

Judith insisted on accompanying her to her room, brushing aside Miss Cartwright's solicitous enquiries in so brusque a fashion as to oblige that young lady to seek her own bedchamber without further protest.

As she kissed Judith goodnight Miss Routledge begged her not to allow *any* of the night's happenings to disturb her rest. In this well-intentioned wish, however, she was to be disappointed for Miss Hammerton lay long awake, wrestling with her unhappy thoughts.

Her deep regard for Rodney Nairn had so long been a part of her, hardly to be spoken of, yet always constant, that she found the very idea of losing him now to be quite insupportable. Had he been killed in battle, or taken a wife during his five years absence from her, then she would have accepted her loss, if not with complacency, at least with a show of resignation, and might even, in time, have turned to another in his stead. But now the case was very different, for the real Rodney Nairn so surpassed her youthful notion of him that she could almost laugh to think what a cardboard caricature she had kept fresh in her memory. And he was not indifferent to her, of that she was reasonably certain. Yet, when the cards were down, who was she, Judith Hammerton, to compare with Georgiana Cartwright, a lady of breeding and position, one of his own world, named for the lovely duchess whose godchild she had been? No, he would surely be looking higher for a wife than one who had only a pretty face and her father's money to commend her.

These sad reflections induced in Miss Hammerton a mood of depression rare in one of so sanguine a temperament, and the first fingers of dawn were plucking at the curtains before she could compose her mind for sleep.

*　　*　　*

The morning saw Lord Penston carry out his avowed intention of removing the Viscount to Netherdene. Miss Cartwright thereupon declared her determination of accompanying her wagon to Fairacre and of removing herself thither as soon as all was made ready for her. Judith accepted her plans with perfect civility but without protest or attempt to persuade her to prolong her stay at the Old Hall. Miss Routledge who, to her own alarm, found herself regretting Rodney's departure less on the score of his receiving inferior attention at Netherdene than because of the possibility that Lord Penston might not find it convenient to make such frequent calls at the Old Hall as he had of late, could not but be relieved that the cause of friction between the two young women had, for the time being at least, been set aside.

On one count she need not have concerned herself, for Lord Penston paid a daily call as punctiliously as ever he had done when Rodney lay at the Old Hall, but almost a week passed before the Viscount was sufficiently recovered to accompany him and then it was on the very day that Miss Cartwright was about to leave for her father's house.

It was an animated party that gathered in the saloon that morning, for their numbers had been augmented by the presence of Mr Geoffrey Woolcott, who had called to pay his respects to the ladies. Mr Woolcott had made a short stay at Brighton earlier in the year, and all those willing to listen were favoured with his opinions of that fashionable resort and how he had been presented to the Prince Regent, and what His Royal Highness had said to him.

'A very obliging sort of man I found him to be, most affable and not above being pleased with his company. The Princess Charlotte, now,' went on this oracle, 'is a bouncy kind of young woman. I should not wonder at it if Coburg found her a bit too much for his patience.'

'What can you mean by that, Mr Woolcott?' enquired Miss Cartwright to whom he was addressing himself. He shrugged delicately, thereby almost doing himself an injury by reason of his preposterously high starched shirt points.

'Oh, to be sure, I meant nothing at all! To be forever profound is quite a bore, you know! But one must say something.'

This piece of modish rudeness so outraged Lord Penston that he remarked in a disgusted aside to Miss Routledge: 'Young jackanapes! Laced up like a lady and smelling like a civet cat! One might be pardoned for doubting his gender!'

Miss Routledge, trying with difficulty to conceal her mirth, hushed him gently. 'It is all an affectation, you know, he is only a boy.' Then, raising her voice a little, she said: 'Did you find His Highness in good health, Mr Woolcott?'

'As to that, ma'am, there's no knowing, for he was wheeling himself about the Pavilion in his Merlin chair by day, while by night he was as merry as a grig and moving as spry as you like.'

'Whatever is a Merlin chair?' Judith begged to know, and Mr Woolcott was pleased to inform her that it was a wheeled contraption invented by some Belgian fellow. He continued his discourse in some detail for his less enlightened hearers until interrupted by Miss Cartwright, who declared she must be on her way for the horses had been walked up and down these twenty minutes and, if she knew anything of Chilcot, she would presently have word from him that he had worn out more shoe leather than she would have done had she gone on foot to Bishop's Stortford.

At that, everybody in the party had to go outside to set her upon her journey and, touching her whip to her very dashing tricorne hat, she urged her fretting horse down the drive, followed by her carriage, driven at a sedate pace by her groom and piled high with baggage, from the midst of which peered the smiling face of her maid and from which emanated the raucous tones of her parrot, adjuring the groom to look sharp and get over the ground if it broke his neck.

In the midst of the parting quips and injunctions few of the party noticed that their numbers were augmented by the arrival of Mr Jasper Edgecombe, who emerged from the Home Wood astride Trumpeter. As Judith, laughing, turned towards the house, she was surprised to find him beside her.

'I am glad I was in time to witness that departure,' he remarked appreciatively. 'But you will miss her company sorely, will you not, ma'am?'

'Who would not?' she countered swiftly, meeting his look with one as blandly innocent. Unlike others of the company, she felt neither partiality nor aversion for Mr Edgecombe. He had a ready wit and a lively mind, and the fact of the Old Hall lying directly on his way from Thaxted to Netherdene provided adequate excuse for his frequent calls upon her, or so it might be supposed. He was, he had informed her, well acquainted with her father, having met that gentleman on several occasions during his visits over the past five years, and seemed particularly wishful to know when he might expect to see Mr Hammerton again.

Judith, who had often wondered what her father's prime object in acquiring the Old Hall might have been, had tried to discover from Mr Edgecombe what common bond of interest lay between him and Mr Hammerton. But Mr Edgecombe was as adroit at dodging her questions as she was at framing them, leaving her with the uncomfortable feeling that he knew very well what she was about and had not the least intention of gratifying her curiosity.

As they turned to re-enter the house, she could not help but observe how his eyes rested speculatively upon Rodney and also how he himself was being observed, though more discreetly, by Lord Penston. Happily, Mr Woolcott's pretentious conversation served to divert the company and relieve the vague air of tension which seemed to have descended upon them.

CHAPTER NINE

MRS WOOLCOTT had set back the date of her dinner party in order that the Viscount might be sufficiently recovered to attend, and found to her chagrin that, by so doing, she had foregone the pleasure of Miss Cartwright's company. As Mr Jasper Edgecombe was now to be included, in order to round off her numbers she issued a gracious invitation to Miss Routledge to accompany Miss Hammerton.

The Woolcott mansion was an imposing one, furnished in a somewhat ornate style but with some fine pieces which owed their origin to the sound taste of the late Mr Woolcott. This gentleman, Judith gathered from her hostess's ready conversation, had been a country squire with a more than comfortable dependance.

'So my boys, you understand, have no need to be on the catch for heiresses — though there is no denying that a wife with a handsome portion is a considerable asset to a young man.'

Thus she prosed on to Lord Penston, and Judith, on his other hand, wondered how much of this artless prattle was directed at her as a way of making it clear that, should she be distinguished by an offer from either Mr Geoffrey or Mr Edward Woolcott, such an honour would not be bestowed upon her by reason of her expectations, however welcome such an infusion into the Woolcott coffers might be.

When the *truites au bleu à la Provençale*, the braised ham with *sauce Madère*, the roast capons with tarragon and other delicacies of the first course had been removed, an even more formidable array of dishes took their place, the chief of which was a handsome saddle of lamb, flanked by mushrooms stewed in champagne, a purée of haricots, new potatoes, and broccoli masked by a cheese sauce. Judith joined with Miss Edgecombe in partaking of an omelette with truffles, followed by a soufflé of apricots, while the dowager was heard to declare loudly that she never saw any reason to have more than two or three side dishes at any course and would be well satisfied with a lemon sorbet and a morsel of cheese.

This reproof from her chief guest Mrs Woolcott took in good part, replying archly that her ladyship's dainty appetite was common knowledge but there were the gentlemen to be thought on, adding aside to Penston: 'Come, confess, my lord, it is a greater set-out than any that has been offered you at Netherdene!' which put his lordship in the difficult position of either replying truthfully and gratifying his hostess's vanity, or of praising the tedious meals invariably set before her guests by Lady Quendon to a degree far beyond their worth.

To Judith's amusement, he steered with effortless skill between the Scylla and Charybdis of these two extremes, and her eye caught the Viscount's merry one in mutually shared appreciation of the carefully turned reply.

'Ma'am, I venture to suspect that you have the advantage of her ladyship hidden away in your kitchens belowstairs. Unless I am much mistaken these confections are the work of an artist.'

Mrs. Woolcott was delighted at his perspicacity and would have regaled him with a detailed account of how she had turned her brother-in-law round her thumb by persuading him to lend her his chef had not the attention of the table been centred upon her younger son who, at the dowager's gracious request, was recounting his impressions of the marriage of the Princess Charlotte to Prince Leopold of Saxe-Coburg.

'Do not, ladies, I pray you, expect me to go into any great detail of dress! I protest I am no man-milliner!' he declared. 'Her Highness was all in silver and white, agleam with diamonds — a most handsome necklace and earrings, given her, I understand, by the Regent, and a diamond bracelet from her husband. But, doubtless, your father will have written you of the occasion and been able to describe it in greater detail than I,' he added, turning to Judith.

'My father?' she echoed, in surprise.

'Yes, for I saw him quite near to me — there is no mistaking his commanding height, is there?'

As the attention of all had been directed upon Mr Woolcott his words were clearly audible down the length of the table. Judith glanced at Miss Routledge who was staring at the young man, her fork arrested in mid-air, her lips parted to receive a succulent mouthful of lamb. Then she observed that Mr Jasper Edgecombe, seated between Miss Routledge and Euphrasia, was also staring at Mr Woolcott and the tense expression on his face gave her cause for wonder.

'Oh, my father is no great letter-writer,' she said quickly to smooth over the awkward moment, 'but as we are in daily expectation of his arrival we shall have it all at first hand from him before very long.'

'If not we shall be forced to journey to London to take him in charge!' put in Miss Routledge, ably seconding her. 'It can afford him no pleasure to be chancing his pot-luck in Bury Street, with only the porter and his man to attend him.'

'If that is your serious intention then allow me to be your escort, ma'am,' said Lord Penston, deftly turning the attention of the company from a subject that appeared to be not quite pleasing to the ladies of the Old Hall. 'I am obliged to return to London not later than the day following to-morrow, since I left for a stay of not more than two days and have been here for close on two weeks.'

At that the dowager was loud in protest at being deprived of her distinguished guest, but his lordship was adamant, pointing out that that Viscount was now able to fend for himself and could the more readily complete the inspection of his estates if left alone than if hindered by the necessity of having to entertain his godfather. Rodney did not look best pleased at this turn of events and privately resolved to terminate his visit to Netherdene in as few days as possible, for the prospect of being en famille with only the dowager and Miss Euphrasia for company held no great attraction for him.

After dinner, when the gentlemen had joined the ladies in the drawing-room, the dowager declared her preference for a rubber of whist. Lord Penston, Mr Edgecombe and Miss Routledge were pressed into obliging her ladyship, while the other members of the party gathered around the fire at the farther end of the room. Presently Lady Quendon called out to them in her authoritative way, and for all the world as if she was the lady of the house.

'Do not any of you young people care for music? I can assure you it will not cause us the least inconvenience. Euphrasia, have you not brought your songs? I am persuaded Quendon will be kind enough to turn over the sheets for you if you will oblige us.'

Miss Edgecombe hastily begged to be excused on the score of having an irritation of the throat. However, when further pressed by her mama and Mrs Woolcott, she consented to display her proficiency upon the pianoforte and executed several pieces in a perfectly correct style but without the least animation or feeling.

Rodney, who had not taken Lady Quendon's hint, but had remained seated by Judith's side, now turned to her to ask if she would favour the party with a display of her talents. She shook her head.

'No, my lord, my performance after that of Miss Edgecombe would give very little satisfaction, I fear.'

'I can engage for it that you will have at least one pair of attentive ears, Miss Hammerton,' he said so earnestly that she coloured up and, when appealed to by her hostess, rose and went to the instrument. 'Have you music?' he asked, following her. 'May I fetch it for you?'

'No, indeed, I must play from memory — and be it upon your own head, my lord, if my fingering goes awry!' she warned him, sitting down upon the music-stool and laying her hands lightly upon the keys.

The Viscount placed himself in a chair at her side to the extreme mortification of Lady Quendon, who remarked in a very ill-tempered way that it was unkind indeed to persuade Miss Hammerton to play after her daughter's excellent performance and, for her part, she could only hope that the young lady would not be put quite out of countenance by so mortifying an experience. Miss Routledge was about to speak out in defence of her charge's abilities when she caught Penston's quizzical look and subsided, while Lady Quendon kindly informed Mr Edgecombe how he might have played the last hand to better advantage. Penston, whose deal it was, held the cards firmly clasped in his hands and, despite her ladyship's injunction to continue with the game, sat with downbent head, listening to Judith.

Hers was a well-trained voice, not great in volume, but making up for that deficiency by its sweetness and depth of expression, while her playing was sufficiently talented to make the whole a most creditable performance. Her appearance, too, in a tiffany gown of a misty, forget-me-not blue, was so engaging that it was only to be expected her song should be greeted with fervent enthusiasm, in particular by the gentlemen, who beseeched her to favour them with further proof of her accomplishments. This she did in a prettily modest way, singing two more ballads with so lively a sense of feeling as to set feet tapping to the music. Then, as she rose and was about to close down the lid of the pianoforte, Rodney, who had been glancing through various sheets of songs, held one out to her with an enquiring expression on his face.

She took it from him and smiled. 'Oh, rare Ben Jonson!' she murmured. 'Many times have I sung this with my father who quite dotes upon it.'

'If I might take his place?' The colour rose to her cheeks again as the double significance of his remark occurred to her and, without another word, she sat down again and struck the opening chords.

A cloud of disapproval descended upon Lady Quendon's brow.

'A song now and then is very desirable,' she complained, 'but it is the misfortune of musical enthusiasts generally that, once beginning, they seldom know when to leave off. There are few things a greater *seccatura* than a long duet upon the pianoforte or an Air with endless Variations.'

Rodney's pleasing light baritone blended so perfectly with Judith's pure tones that even Lady Quendon left off protesting and sat, without uttering a word, in unwilling appreciation of the charming duet. When the last notes had died away there was such an outburst of applause that Rodney was startled into taking his eyes off Judith's lovely face in order to acknowledge the acclaim being accorded them. Mrs Woolcott was heard to declare that nothing like it could be heard at Covent Garden, though Mr Edgecombe showed no sign of having heard a note of the performance and Lord Penston wondered at his abstraction even as he protested he had seldom listened to anything he liked half so well.

'Indeed, Quendon has a very pretty voice,' conceded the dowager. 'Which, of its excellence, conceals the imperfections of his companion's.'

'I'll take issue with you there, ma'am, said Penston, at last yielding to her importunities and dealing the cards. 'My godson's voice provides the perfect foil for Miss Hammerton's clarity of tone. Rarely, even in the highest professional circles, have I heard such exquisite harmony.'

He looked towards the group standing about the pianoforte as he spoke and observed Rodney raise Judith's hand to his lips, as if in homage. Despite their being surrounded by voluble Woolcotts and an engagingly delighted Euphrasia, there was something strangely remote about their two figures, a particularity that seemed to set them apart from their companions. He glanced at Miss Routledge and saw from her expression that she felt as he did.

'"Drink to me only with thine eyes" — indeed!' he quoted softly, and they exchanged a smile of understanding which, being perceived by Lady Quendon, earned them the tart reminder that she was still waiting to resume play.

Despite protestations from their hosts, the party broke up predictably early when the dowager had played sufficient rubbers of whist. The gentlemen were all eager to offer themselves as escort to the Old Hall, but Miss Routledge declared that Chilcot was a match for any lurking footpad, and they drove away with the pleasantest impressions of an evening that had not promised half so well at the outset.

*   *   *

Once alone together, they at once fell to discussion of Mr Hammerton's odd behaviour.

'Can we be certain that it was your father that Mr Edward saw? How well does he know him?'

'Better, I collect, than most people in these parts for he was used to run wild in our woods as a lad and so continued the practice after the change of owner. My father, on one of his visits here, caught him out and, so Edward freely confessed to me, gave him a teazing, but afterwards he forgave him his fault and granted him the freedom of the grounds just so long as he did not disturb the birds.'

'But,' said Miss Routledge, unconvinced, 'it is a full week since Her Royal Highness was wed.'

'It is all of that,' agreed Judith. 'For, if you remember, Georgy told us how the town was agog in expectation of the event when she arrived in London.'

The two ladies were silent for a moment, then Miss Routledge said quietly: 'I should have thought it possible for Mr Hammerton to have sent word of his coming but, no doubt, he has much business to attend to and could not be sure how soon it might be concluded.'

'He knows perfectly well that we would be only too happy to come to town and open up Bury Street for his convenience. No, I am persuaded he does not wish his presence made known.' Miss Routledge, who was of the same opinion, ventured to suggest that it might be wiser to feign ignorance until Mr Hammerton chose to communicate with them. 'I cannot be sure,' confessed Judith. 'I — I wonder if Georgy knew anything of his plans.'

'That is easily resolved,' said Miss Routledge. 'Pay her a call to-morrow morning and ask her.'

'Yes, I dare say I could do that,' replied Judith a trifle absently, for her thoughts were less with her father and Miss Cartwright at that moment than dwelling on whether the Viscount might, perhaps, accompany Lord Penston back to London and whether she had read too much meaning into his marked attentions that evening.

Miss Routledge, who had a very fair notion of what was passing through the young lady's mind, gently cleared her throat and said hesitantly: 'Gentlemen, you must know, my dear, have many more interests in life than are granted to us poor creatures. Your father —'

'My father is still quite a young and vigorous man — no older, I would imagine, than Lord Penston?'

Miss Routledge was grateful for the darkness that hid her blushes. 'No, I fancy they are of an age,' she replied composedly.

Judith chuckled. 'Fie upon you, Miss Patience! Are you suggesting that papa may have some fair Cyprian in attendance, hence his wishing to be private?'

'I am not suggesting anything of the kind!' said Miss Routledge tartly. 'And it is most improper, let me tell you, for his daughter to make any such animadversions about Mr Hammerton.'

'Then, if you please, what can be in your mind?' asked Judith, quite unabashed by the reproof.

'Have you never thought that your father might wish to marry again? That he may have held back from doing so by consideration of your feelings, not wishing to burden you with a stepmother, and hoping you might have set up your own establishment before such a situation arose?'

'No,' admitted Judith. 'I confess I had not thought of any such thing.'

'Then I advise you to do so,' said Miss Routledge, hating herself for such forthright talk but being assured that, in this instance, it was more cruel to be kind. While her own suspicions could well be pure conjecture yet she was of the opinion that Judith should be prepared in some fashion for such an eventuality. 'If you are truly persuaded that your best course would be to return to London,' she went on as she prepared to alight from the carriage, 'then I must busy myself to-morrow in setting the household affairs to rights lest our stay in Bury Street should be of some duration.'

Judith made no answer and Miss Routledge, observing her preoccupation, forebore to trouble her with further discussion of their plans.

*   *   *

Meantime, Rodney, having dismissed his valet, was just

about to snuff out the candles and get into bed when the sound of a voice uttering his name low outside caused him to call out in question: 'Yes?'

To his astonishment the door opened to admit Mr Edgecombe.

'I allow it to be an infamous hour of night to be troubling you, Quendon,' said that gentleman in the most friendly manner imaginable, 'but if we might have a few moments of private conversation I am assured that much that may appear somewhat obscure to you could be — er, made plain.'

Rodney sighed and shrugged on his dressing-robe again. 'Pray be seated,' he said, barely suppressing a yawn. 'But I warn you that, had you called five minutes later, I should have been under the covers and sound asleep.'

'I promise you that what I have to say, my lord, is most likely to put all thought of sleep from your mind.' Mr Edgecombe was all civility, but there was that in his regard which the Viscount found more than a little disquieting.

'Would a glass of brandy help you to tell your tale?' he enquired, breaking the taut silence that fell after his visitor's last remark.

'If you will join me.'

'By your tone, it appears you think it likely that I may need it.'

'You well may,' agreed Mr Edgecombe, accepting the brandy offered him with a slight bow.

'Then give me leave to charge my glass!' Rodney spoke half in jest, but he was fully sensible that the situation could prove to be far from diverting. 'Your health, cousin!'

'Your health, my lord. How is it with your arm? Do you still suffer pain?'

'Not unless I am forgetful enough to attempt to lift something with it. But you are not here to enquire after my injury, are you?'

'It was not I who shot you, you know,' said Mr Edgecombe casually.

'I did not suppose that you had,' returned Rodney, equally cool.

'But you will allow that the weight of opinion was against me?'

'Understandably so. Your motive for wishing me out of the way was lamentably clear. If you were not the culprit, do you know who was?'

'I could hazard a guess but will content myself with suggesting that it was not you that drew the marksman's fire, but your horse.'

'Trumpeter? But why?'

'I should say more precisely, *my* horse.' Mr Edgecombe extended one shapely leg to the fire and appeared to be lost in contemplation of his blue and white striped silk stockings. Rodney watched him closely.

'Are you telling me that I was fired upon in mistake for you?'

Mr Edgecombe swirled the brandy about in his glass, watching the golden liquid sparkle in the firelight. 'I have not lived for close on thirty years without making enemies,' was all he said, and Rodney was put irresistibly in mind of his father. So very like Sir Rollo, he reflected, to refuse to be conciliatory, even to take a perverse pleasure in arousing antagonism in others. Why had he not perceived this side of his cousin's nature? Mr Edgecombe answered that question for him as if he had spoken aloud. 'You had not thought me to be that sort of man, had you?' he asked softly. 'But you can be sure I have enemies.'

'Why would any one of them attempt to kill you?'

'Perhaps it was feared that if a period was not put to my existence, I might well do that service for you.'

'You are not suggesting that Lord Penston—'

'Good God, no!' Jasper Edgecombe laughed outright at the very notion. 'His lordship would never shoot a sitting bird! It is always a great pleasure to be dealing with gentlemen, they are so very predictable.'

The scorn implicit in his voice stung Rodney to retort. 'And you do not regard yourself as such?'

'A bastard is only a gentleman by courtesy of his friends — if friends he has.'

'A bastard?' Rodney stared at him, uncomprehending.

'Yes, my lord. Though my father was not, in the literal sense of the word, a bastard, unhappily, I am.'

Rodney set down his glass. 'Let me understand you,' he said carefully. 'Are you saying that your mother's husband was not your father?'

'I am saying that *your* mother's husband *was* my father! He laughed again at Rodney's expression of stunned disbelief. 'Well met, little brother!'

CHAPTER
TEN

MR EDGECOMBE'S revelation, as was to be expected, left Rodney feeling as shaken as if he had been planted a facer until his new-found brother's voice recalled him to as sense of reality.

'You had not suspected?'

'I ought to have done, I suppose, but my father had changed greatly in appearance these latter years.' On an impulse, he held out his hand. 'We have neither of us much to thank him for — Jasper.'

After an instant's hesitation, Mr Edgecombe clasped the proffered hand. 'No, nor had our mothers. He deserted mine the moment he heard of my coming and, in large part due to the combined efforts of my grandfather and the late Lord Quendon, she was married off to a cousin, a simpleton, who was so overjoyed at being presented with a son that he never thought to count on the fingers of one hand!'

'So Lord Quendon knew of my father's share in the business?'

'Aye, and despised me for it! As my likeness to Sir Rollo increased with the years so did Quendon's hatred of me grow. Oh, he never mentioned it openly, but he had a fondness for my mother and never forgave — our father for what he did. She was a soft, pretty woman, as feather-witted as you please, but appealing to the male taste. Such were my parents and I had to make the best of them. Your mother was a very different sort of lady.'

'You knew her?'

'I met her once, the only time that I ever saw our father put out of countenance. He had summoned me to attend him at his house in London, saying it would be perfectly safe since you were at school and Lady Mary away, visiting friends.

Unhappily, she returned when I was bidding him farewell in the hall. The resemblance must have struck her like a blow between the eyes and, for once, our father's smooth tongue failed him. She recovered herself quickly enough, seeing my confusion, and spoke to me graciously, but the damage had been done. I was a mere stripling and had not the wit to extricate myself with ease from such a situation, but she dismissed me kindly, saying I must come again to meet *her* boy — you, Quendon. Needless to say, I did not, and I heard of her death just over a year later.'

'So that was what caused the rift between them,' said Rodney slowly. 'She was devoted to him until then.'

'I'd not willingly have caused her pain.' Jasper's voice was rough with feeling. 'She was a sweet lady.'

Rodney looked at him in some wonder. 'Why are you telling me all this? It may well be, even yet, that you could succeed after me.'

'You don't imagine I'd set my name to it in writing, do you?' sneered Mr Edgecombe. 'And let me tell you that if you had been another such as your father —' He turned away abruptly to look into the fire and continued speaking in an oddly subdued voice. 'You are as like to your mother as is possible for a man.'

Rodney had to force himself to break the silence that fell between them. 'Sir Rollo did not then utterly cast you off?'

'Not when he found I might be of use to him. When my grandfather died I was past sixteen and, knowing his end was near and that Lord Quendon would do nothing for me, my mother appealed to Sir Rollo to aid her in setting me up, for my legal father was, by that time, little more than an imbecile. So I was offered a clerking position in the counting house of one, Mr George Hammerton, a merchant of the City of London.'

'What?' Rodney could hardly believe his ears. 'Does Miss Hammerton know of this?'

'Not through me and I doubt her father has told her. I was not in his employ for many months for, being born and bred to a country way of life, the place stifled me. Then it was decided that I might be of more use living at the Old Hall and receiving the cargoes.'

'The cargoes?' echoed the mystified Rodney.

'Where are your wits, my lord?' Mr Edgecombe taunted him, but not unkindly. 'Did you not know that our father and Hammerton worked between them the neatest smuggling confederacy in the country? The sprawling cellars of the Old Hall were a perfect repository for such dangerous merchandise, unsuspected by anyone and too far from the coast to excite the interest of the exciseman. That is why I was in the passage a week ago, seeing to the unblocking of the cellar door. There is still a fine store of brandy down there and I am running low at Thaxted. I am sorry I caused alarm to Miss Cartwright, but I conceived the notion of looking in on you and telling you something of this story then. Was it Penston's idea to guard you so closely?'

'No, it was Miss Cartwright's.'

'So?' Mr Edgecombe raised his eyebrows in mock dismay. 'The lady does not trust me?'

'The lady is newly come from Lisbon where she met Mr Hammerton, who warned her that I could be in danger.'

'And who himself was seen in London over a week ago, yet has not announced his arrival to his devoted daughter,' mused Mr Edgecombe. 'Yes, the fragments of the puzzle are all falling into place.'

'Then explain me this,' said the Viscount crisply. 'Were you also re-stocking your cellar when you shut Miss Routledge into the passage on the night following your visit to my room?'

'What can you mean?' Rodney told him briefly what had taken place. 'It was not I but — yes, it is all of a piece. He must have come here straight upon arrival from Lisbon — or both of them, perhaps.'

'Both of whom, for God's sake?' demanded the mystified Rodney.

'George Hammerton and our father.'

'Sir Rollo? He is still alive, then?'

'To my certain knowledge, he was until a few months ago, hid away in Jamaica. He may still be there, but I think it unlikely. Once recovered of his wound, he's come back to find me. I was the one who set the hounds on his track, he'd not easily forgive that. He would also want to be sure that you were aware of his continued existence and so be troubled by the knowledge that you stood in his shoes.'

'How well you know him,' said Rodney in an oddly expressionless voice. 'Yet I think there is much you have not told me. How did he come by his wound? And what did you mean by saying that you had put the hounds on his track?'

'Oh, as to his being wounded,' explained Mr Edgecombe airily, 'that was an unfortunate thing. In endeavouring to slip away unobserved from Brussels, he was involved in an unlikely fracas — well, perhaps, not unlikely when one considers the lovely lightskirt he had in keeping. A pretty piece of goods she was, 'pon my honour.'

'I know,' retorted Rodney, feeling any mention of Mr Edgecombe's honour to be singularly inapt. 'I called upon her when pursuing my enquiries in Brussels last year.'

Mr Edgecombe's eyes widened in surprise. 'Did you so? And, I'll wager, you learned no more from her than would sit upon a farthing.'

'Was there anything to learn? Is not that pretty head of hers as empty as a dandelion clock?'

'That young female,' said Mr Edgecombe deliberately, 'is, or was, one of the most needle-witted spies in Bonaparte's pay.'

'What? Did my father know of this?'

The other reflected for a little before making reply. 'He doted upon her — oh, it comes to us all, even to such as Sir Rollo, the fear of failing powers, the desperate need for assurance — that, I fancy, was how it all began. But she had other and very different aims. Our well-established free-trading enterprise was tailored to fit her designs of sending and receiving snippets of information. I cannot say when first he found out how he was being used but, by then, it was far too late. His involvement and that of Hammerton was unquestioned, his to a vastly greater degree for she had arranged for letters to be written, mentioning him by name.'

'And she used these against him? Did he not threaten to reveal her activities?'

'And so pull down Hammerton and himself with her,

innocent though they were of any treachery? Who would believe them? No, Sir Rollo had to do what he was bid — nor, I am persuaded, did he find it too uncomfortable, for it was uncommon well-paid, and he had much of the lady's attention.'

'But not all?'

'Oh, she called the tune, have no doubt of that! In crude cant, dear brother, she was a leary flash mot, a devilish knowing one and, as I found to my delight, well versed in her trade!' Mr Edgecombe smiled reminiscently. 'That gave me some satisfaction, I can tell you!' The look of revulsion on the Viscount's face seemed to afford him considerable amusement. 'Much too nice in your sensibilities, Quendon. I wonder at it after five years in the Peninsula.' He drained his glass and rose. 'I confess I pleased the lady well, and so sympathetic did she find me to her aims that she showed me those letters that set our father outside the law — indeed, made me free of them.'

'So it was you who betrayed him?'

'You could put it that way,' agreed Mr Edgecombe. 'But consider, before condemning me, that I removed one obstacle from your path to becoming Viscount Quendon.'

'Let me set this out clearly.' The Viscount, brows knitted in thought, began to pace about the room while Mr Edgecombe leaned, quite at his ease, one arm propped negligently against the mantelshelf, observing him. 'You made yourself known to the woman my — our father had in keeping and persuaded her to give you certain papers that showed positive proof of his guilt — though guilty he was not, save perhaps in continuing to countenance the treachery. These papers you later sent to the British authority so that Sir Rollo should be branded as a traitor did he ever show his face in public again.'

'Most admirably expressed,' approved Mr Edgecombe, 'but for one small point, which I feel I ought to mention. The lady did not precisely *give* me the letters, I — er, acquired them.'

'You mean, you stole them?'

Mr Edgecombe sighed. 'Crudely put, but true enough.'

The Viscount said nothing but waited for him to continue.

'The lady discovered her loss and knew well on whom to lay the blame for it. It did not suit her plans to have suspicion fall on Sir Rollo at that time as he was known to be a familiar of hers, so she devised a cunning trap to pay me out in my own coin by inviting me to visit her while he disported himself at the Richmond's ball on the eve of Waterloo, then privily sending him word that the letters had been stolen and he had best look to his safety.'

Rodney stared at him in mounting apprehension. 'So he returned to find you in possession?'

'Oh, at home to a peg', nodded Mr Edgecombe. 'Which put him, as you may imagine, completely at Point-Non-Plus. Then he flew into a fury and drew a sword upon me, which had the lady in a taking, for a scandal in her lodging was the last thing she desired. She was, I am assured, in full expectation of Sir Rollo's settling my score for me but, unhappily for her, he tripped over a trailing gown or cast-off shoe or some such and my blade entered deep between his ribs. I thought him past praying for, I can tell you, but between us we contrived to patch him up and set the room to rights. I knew where Hammerton was lodged in Brussels and urged my fair Paphian to send at once to him.'

'How did he get away?' Rodney asked.

'Oh, Hammerton took him in charge and hid him away until he was sufficiently recovered to take ship for Jamaica.'

'Why did Hammerton quit the country, too?'

'I fancy it was because he had no notion of what I intended. If I had in mind openly to accuse my father then his associates would be hard put to it to prove their innocence. I, of course, would be turning King's Evidence and could claim the leniency of the law, though there was little enough to connect me with any of it.'

'Can this be why Hammerton is keeping himself so secret in London?'

'No.' Mr Edgecombe was very definite on that point. 'Had I wished to bring him down I would have done it long since. The letters I sent to the British authority involved only my father. Had they pursued the matter deeply then, no doubt, Hammerton's connection with the business would have been revealed but, believing Sir Rollo to be dead, they allowed the affair to rest. I have no quarrel with Hammerton. He is innocent of any ill intent towards me — at least, he was. Now, I am not perfectly sure of his benevolence.'

'What, then, do you suppose is his intention?'

'To kill me if he can,' said Mr Edgecombe calmly. 'Or assist our precious parent in that aim. My death will not clear Sir Rollo's name but it will salve his pride and put his mind at ease on your account. Think how galling it would be for papa to have me installed at Netherdene as the Viscount Quendon while he skulked about the lesser-known places of the earth, unable to show his face! Now,' he finished up briskly, 'I must be gone and you to your bed, though I doubt to sleep!'

When Mr Edgecombe had left him, Rodney sank into a chair and sat, chin on hand, staring into the still glowing embers of the fire, endeavouring to sort his thoughts into some semblance of order. What right had he to censure his brother? God knew Jasper had reason enough — but to brand his father as a traitor stuck in the throat. Yet for all that he was as like to Sir Rollo as two coats cut from the same cloth, there was a kindness in Jasper that was markedly lacking in his progenitor. If, of course, fortune or the devil should take a hand and remove the young brother who stood between him and the title, then Rodney could readily visualise Mr Edgecombe's philosophical shrug of the shoulders and perfect willingness to accept what offered. No sentiment about brother Jasper but, he felt reasonably assured, save in the one instance, no premeditated malice either.

An incautious movement of his arm as he rose from his chair reminded him acutely of his wound. Who had fired that shot? Hammerton? Or Sir Rollo, aiming to kill one son in order to save the other? Rodney's lips twisted wryly. That would be the most famous thing, if it were true! Sir Rollo seeking his revenge, more like.

'God, what a coil!' he muttered as he flung himself into bed and, closing his eyes, prayed for sleep to calm his agitated mind.

*   *   *

Alone in his room, Mr Edgecombe, who had not thought to

bring his valet with him for so brief a stay, eased himself out of his admirably fitting coat and modish waistcoat. He then surveyed his reflection in the tall cheval-glass with some complacency.

'Not at all despicable,' he decided. 'Showing a trifle heavy about the waistline but nothing to signify. That young brother of yours, now, is a handsome creature, and when the scales are weighed down in his favour with a title, his suit is most likely to prosper.' He paced about the room for a time, deep in meditation, before seating himself at a secretary and drawing a sheet of hot-pressed paper — one of Lady Quendon's rare extravagances — towards him. 'No,' he contined on the same reflective note, dipping his pen into the standish, 'I am sorry for the young lovers, but it will be a test of their resolution. I only hope I do not find myself at daggersdrawing with brother Rodney which, I must confess, seems very likely! As our good Jackson so often is heard to declare "whoever is not for you is against you, mill away right and left"!' He chuckled softly. 'To which I would add "and use whatever weapon comes nearest to hand"!'

CHAPTER
ELEVEN

THE ladies of the Old Hall were sitting down to breakfast when Mr Edgecombe's note was delivered by his groom.

'I declare this could not have fallen out better,' said Judith, to whom it was addressed. 'Mr Edgecombe has also conceived the notion of calling upon Georgy to-day and asks if either or both of us would care to accompany him. He will call here at ten o'clock to discover our wishes. He does stress that three in a curricle for so great a journey might be a shade uncomfortable!'

'Which puts me in my place!' remarked Miss Routledge tartly. 'Oh, dear, I *do* dislike this expanding toast-rack! It is so apt to scatter the toast all about the table. I thought I had told Jessop to put it away.'

'If you take it firmly — so,' said Judith, suiting action to words, 'it behaves in a perfectly reasonable manner. Dare I accuse you of being a shade mifty this morning, dear Miss Patience?'

'There are so many things to be thought on if we are to go to London to-morrow,' sighed Miss Routledge in a slightly distracted way, 'and there are cards to be left at Woolcott Manor — one each to our host and hostess should suffice, do you not think?'

'Yes, but be sure to turn down a corner for Edward, he is quite my favourite of that family. And Chilcot can perform that office for you as I shall not be requiring him now.'

'Yes — Judith, had you best not make haste? It is past nine o'clock already.'

Judith calmly spread more quince preserve over her toast. 'Georgy thought the journey from here to be near fifteen miles,' she said meditatively. 'If one adds on the four traversed in coming from Netherdene, then Mr Edgecombe will have need to bait his horses. He drives a pair, not a team, I believe.'

'It will take the best part of two hours,' agreed Miss Routledge.

'Doubtless, Georgy will give us a nuncheon to revive our flagging spirits.'

'You'll not be back before four o'clock,' prophesied Miss Routledge despondently. 'Can you give me any hint of what gowns you had thought to take with you to-morrow, so that I may set Sarah to pressing and folding them?'

'Not many, I think.' Judith considered another piece of toast but put the thought firmly from her. 'I had best go upstairs and look them out. Shall Sarah come with us?'

'Lord Penston said he would call to-day to discuss the arrangements.'

'Most obliging of his lordship!' twinkled Judith. 'One would not suppose him to be generally regarded as a proud sort of man — thought to be very full of starch by a number of worthy persons, so I have heard!'

Miss Routledge wisely declined to rise to that fly and advised Miss Hammerton to get on with her breakfast or she would be keeping Mr Edgecombe's horses standing. 'Oh, Jessop, Mr Edgecombe's groom is not waiting for a reply to this letter, is he?'

'No, ma'am,' said Jessop, setting down a fresh pot of coffee. 'With your permission, he will await his master's arrival here. Do I understand miss will not now be requiring the carriage?'

'No, I shall not. Would you please so inform Chilcot?'

'Judith,' said Miss Routledge in a troubled way when the butler had withdrawn, 'I cannot be entirely happy about your going all that way with Mr Edgecombe. I do wish you were taking Chilcot with you.'

'Dear Miss Patience,' laughed Miss Hammerton. 'With his groom standing up behind us and a mettlesome pair to handle, what harm can he do to me?'

'None, I suppose,' allowed Miss Routledge doubtfully. 'But I cannot be quite easy in my mind. And why only Mr Edgecombe? Why does not Quendon accompany him?'

'Because he is occupied with estate business from an early

hour to-day, so he informed me last night. Now confess it! This is all because you have taken poor Mr Edgecombe in dislike, and for what reason?'

'That I do not know,' admitted Miss Routledge. 'But Lord Penston has no great liking for him either and surely his judgement is to be relied upon?'

'By you most certainly!' Judith swiftly bent to kiss her mentor's cheek as she passed behind her chair and was gone before Miss Routledge could rake her down for her impertinence.

Left to herself, she had to allow that there was much truth in her charge's last quip and that the cause of her rare irritation of nerves was Lord Penston himself. Well did she know how very unlikely it was that a man of his consequence, who must be considered past the age of contracting a hasty and unsuitable marriage, would even entertain the idea of offering for her. He was a delightful, personable gentleman and if his attentions to her had been somewhat marked — well, who else was there in their small circle for him to engage in a light flirtation? And she, like any silly girl just out of the schoolroom, had fallen besottedly in love with him, shaken clean out of her customary composure, blinded by his good looks and splendid person, his charm of manner and, most of all, by his kindness to so obscure a creature as a mere companion.

She was still sitting at the table, indulging in what she knew to be improbable daydreams, when Mr Edgecombe's curricle, prompt to time, drew up before the door and Judith, as promptly, came downstairs. Her high-crowned chip straw bonnet was trimmed and secured by ribbons of deep blue velvet that matched her caped pelisse; neat low-heeled walking shoes peeped out from under the deep flounce of her spotted muslin frock and, instead of a reticule, she carried a large swansdown muff, with a tippet of the same draped loosely about her neck. Miss Routledge eyed this vastly becoming get-out with some misgiving.

'If the weather should turn inclement,' she began dubiously.

'I shall require Jessop to place an umbrella in the curricle to forestall such disaster.' Miss Hammerton adjusted her short

Limerick gloves of fine buff-coloured leather. 'Do not be in the fidgets, I beg you, Miss Patience. Should Mr Edgecombe prove to be less a gentleman than we suppose or other mischance befall me, I promise you I shall take myself to the Crown or the Coach and Horses at Hockerill, there board the London mail from Cambridge, and so arrive in Bury Street before you!'

Miss Routledge kissed her fondly. 'You are talking nonsense and I, no doubt, am being over-anxious. Be off with you and have a pleasant day. Give, if you please, my respects to Miss Cartwright.'

The sun was shining from a clear sky and the easterly wind blew light and mild when Mr Edgecombe gave his pair the office to start, his groom swung smartly up behind, and they spurted off at a lively pace. The gentleman was in the highest spirits, the lady willing to be pleased, the countryside showing the fresh and delightful face of early May — nothing, it seemed, could mar their pleasurable anticipation of a day spent in enjoyment and good company. Then Mr Edgecombe announced that he had the intention of calling at the George at Bishop's Stortford.

'There we may change horses for the last four or five miles and pick up my pair on the return, thus saving considerable time.'

Judith had no fault to find with this arrangement and looked about her with interest as they drove into the thriving busy town of Bishop's Stortford. The George Inn was situated in North Street, a fine wide thoroughfare with some handsome buildings to be seen, particularly upon the West side. Mr Edgecombe suggested that the lady step inside for a cup of coffee while a fresh pair was being put to, and he obtained more precise directions about the location of Miss Cartwright's residence.

'Coffee?' she exclaimed as he handed her down from the curricle. 'Why, I can smell it now! I declare they must keep the pot on the boil.'

As a Norwich-bound coach had just drawn out the place was busy with ostlers and her remark occasioned broad grins on many faces.

'Ut don't be coffee, miss,' remarked one greybeard. 'Ut be barley!'

'Barley?' wondered Judith.

'Ah, there be a rare sight o' kilns here. Mind how ye step, miss, th' place is all in a caddle with them coach folk — hey, what's along o' he?'

To her surprise, Judith observed Timson, Mr Edgecombe's groom, picking himself up off the ground in a very uncertain way, and had his master not caught his arm to support him there seemed no doubt that he would have fallen again.

''Tis my knee, sir. I slipped as I got down and caught it a rare owd tap.'

Mr Edgecombe ran an exploratory hand over the injured part. 'That you have,' he owned. 'Miss Hammerton, if you would be so good as to step into the coffee-room — ah, landlord! What can be done for this poor fellow here? I am no bonesetter.'

Judith was half-way through her second cup in the deserted coffee-room when Mr Edgecombe joined her, looking a trifle harassed.

'The landlord, a very good sort of man, has attended to the dislocated joint,' he informed her. 'Timson will do, but it is a nasty wrench and he is in no case to be standing up behind us. If you are in agreement, I suggest we complete the few miles left of the journey and leave him here to rest until our return. It will be something of a crush, I am afraid, back to the Old Hall.'

Judith, thinking of what Miss Routledge would have to say of this unexpected comeabout, could scarce repress a smile. 'Since we are so far on our way, sir, it would seem singularly witless to discontinue our journey now,' she agreed. 'And, so long as I am back at the Old Hall near to four o'clock, what matters it how I get there?'

Mr Edgecombe gallantly kissed her hand and she was obliged to allow he did it with a great deal of style. 'Then, with your permission, we will set out at once, ma'am. The sooner off, the sooner to return.'

She was in full accord with him, but could not refrain from remarking: 'It but remains for Miss Cartwright to be from home to put the cap on our misfortunes!' which caused him to laugh and rally her on her lack of spirit. He then handed her up into the curricle and they threaded their way through the crowded streets, he explaining that it was a fortunate thing he had asked for clear directions, since it appeared that Fairacre lay secluded and at a greater distance from Bishop's Stortford than he had imagined.

'I had thought it to be by Spellbrook, near to the old turnpike gate, for Miss Cartwright spoke of that as being no great way from the house, but I suspect her long sojourn in the Peninsula has given her some irregular notions as to distance and time.'

The curricle was bowling along briskly and Judith was so entertained by her companion's cheerful conversation that it was not until they had left the turnpike road and were proceeding at a more sober pace along a narrow lane between high, flower-dotted hedgerows, that she was moved to protest.

'Are you quite sure, sir, that you know where we are?'

'To be direct with you, ma'am, I am not!' he admitted with disconcerting candour. 'At least, I know where we are at this very moment, but where we stand in relation to Miss Cartwright's house is something of a mystery.'

'And I thought you claimed to know this country better than any!' she teased him, but there was a coolness in her eyes that might have put him on his guard had he observed it.

'Ah!' he cried a moment later, checking the horses down to a walk. 'Here, at least, is somewhere I do know.' She looked in surprise at the cottage nestling in a fold of the ground, surrounded by a well-laid-out garden. 'My old nurse lives here, she'll set us right, but it means that we will have to step inside and pass the time of day with her, she would never forgive me did I not.'

He darted a swift glance from under his lids at Judith but she feigned interest in the prospect that lay before her and answered him lightly. 'As I am persuaded your nurse will take small comfort in talking to me, would it not be best if I walked the horses while you sought her advice? Time is our enemy, Mr Edgecombe, as I have no need to remind you.'

'To be sure,' he agreed as they turned in at a gateway then, tossing her the reins, he leapt nimbly down and went to secure the gate behind them. 'But, as you can see, there is no space in

the lane to be parading the horses up and down, nor any room
to turn.'

The curricle had come to a stand in a trim, cobbled yard,
surrounded by outhouses on two sides, the cottage itself
stretching the length of a third and the gate by which they had
entered flanked by high stone walls on either side, closing the
fourth. As she looked about at the neat little trap into which she
had been driven, the door to the cottage opened and the figure
of an old, white-haired woman stood on the threshold, peering
at them with the intentness of the very short-sighted.

Mr Edgecombe strode forward to clasp her in his arms and
she greeted him with every appearance of joy. This felicitous
scene went far to soothe Judith's suspicions, and when the old
woman came forward to drop her a curtsy and beg her to step
into the house she felt it to be unreasonably churlish to refuse
such a request.

While Mr Edgecombe attended to his horses, she was guided
to a low-beamed parlour where lemonade and biscuits were set
out for her, her hostess clucking and smiling away to herself,
like a happy child with some new plaything. Judith made
several attempts to engage her attention but she seemed unable
to understand any questions asked her and Mr Edgecombe put
an end to the one-sided conversation when he entered the room
and held the door wide for the old woman to leave them. Then
he shut and locked the door behind her, taking the key from the
lock and placing it in his pocket.

This openly declared proof of his intentions evoked no
response from Judith who sipped her lemonade and watched
him, uttering not a word until, at last, he was forced to speak
with grudging admiration.

'You are a cool hand, I must confess, ma'am. I had not
expected a female to show such commendable restraint.'

'Of what use is there to lament, sir? It would appear that you
hold all the aces in the pack.'

He stood, hands on hips, frowning slightly. 'First, believe
me, I regret the necessity for this, but no other course was open
to me. Your father —'

'Ah, I suspected we would come to my father!' she

murmured. 'Tell me, Mr Edgecombe, why are you so wary of him?'

He smiled slightly. 'Because I fancy he is trying to kill me, holding, as he does, the mistaken belief that I am trying to kill Quendon.'

'Which, of course, you are not?'

'Which I most certainly am not. I prefer to be alive and plain Mr Edgecombe than the late Lord Quendon, and so I have told my — the Viscount.' She nodded serenely.

'But you do not expect my father to believe that so you wish to bargain with him, holding me as a hostage?'

His smile broadened. 'I vow it is a real pleasure to be dealing with a lady like yourself whose acuteness of perception is rivalled only by her beauty! I suppose you would not consider marrying me?'

'No, Mr Edgecombe, I would not, but I thank you for your generous offer.'

'Generous it is, ma'am, for if you have to spend a week or more here in my company with only Betsy for propriety, even your father must advise you to accept my proposal.'

'Betsy *is* your old nurse, then?'

'Indeed,' he assented. 'And, apart from being quite deaf and almost blind, she has been astray in her wits these ten years, poor creature.'

'And your groom is in none too bad a case, I dare say?'

'That, I fear, was a necessary deception. I have need of Timson to cover our tracks at the George. He is, I trust, at this moment regaling the staff of that reputable hostelry with a tale that should appeal to their sense of the romantic.'

She raised an enquiring eyebrow. 'Which is, sir?'

'Our elopement, to be sure.'

'Not to Gretna Green!' She threw up her hands in mock horror. 'Spare me that impropriety!'

'No, no, to London, where we are to be married by special licence.'

'I see. May I ask how you propose to inform my father that you have taken possession of my person? Do you know where he is to be found?'

'Not precisely, but I suspect that to be no insurmountable difficulty. If you will be good enough to write a note to Miss Routledge, explaining the unhappy position in which you find yourself, I have no doubt that word of it will get to your father's ears before very long.'

She regarded him thoughtfully. 'Through some member of the household who is in my father's confidence?'

Amusement vied with admiration in his eyes as he watched her. 'So I would imagine.'

She looked about her. 'And, in the meantime, I am to be held prisoner here with you as my gaoler?'

'For that I can only beg your pardon. But do not be afraid, I promise I shall not lay finger on you, your reputation will be damaged in name only, unless of course —' He paused significantly.

'I am not afraid,' she returned, sounding neither defiant nor self-assured, but simply matter-of-fact, 'and can only hope you will present me with a written testimonial confirming my probity of character when this charade is over.'

He laughed. 'I am persuaded a word from me in his lordship's ear will prove sufficient!'

She flashed him a look of acute distaste. 'Be so good as to inform me where I am to sleep to-night.'

'Why here, to be sure.' He flung open a door, revealing a tiny chamber, little bigger than a closet, with a small barred window, its entire space being occupied by a bed and a chair. 'A trifle incommodious, I fear, but necessity must be served. Ah, I hear Betsy calling. No doubt she wishes to know if we will take a nuncheon. By-the-by, save for one small vent, that window does not open.'

When he had let himself out of the room and the key had turned in the lock behind him, she walked to the window at the end of the chamber which looked out upon a pleasant formal garden. An attempt to open the lattices proved the truth of Mr Edgecombe's assertion and she stood there, disconsolate, her mind in a turmoil.

To say that she had been unprepared for such a situation was not strictly true. Despite his friendly attentions, she had had her doubts of Mr Edgecombe for some time past, but had been unable to discover in what way he constituted a threat to her peace of mind. She had long suspected his association with her father to have been more profound than he was prepared to admit and had often wondered what was the whole truth of it, so that Miss Routledge's doubts and anxieties of the morning had aroused a sympathetic echo in her own mind.

Slowly she walked back to the table and, picking up her muff, drew from it a small but serviceable pistol. When she had placed it there earlier in the day, she had been tempted to laugh at her misgivings but now, as she handled it, the coldness of the metal reassured her. Then, shaking her head, she slid it back into its hiding-place.

'Not now,' she mused. 'He is sure to leave the house at some time and then there is only the old woman to contend with and, perhaps, the groom if he returns here.'

Her reflections were interrupted by the entrance of Mr Edgecombe, followed by the old woman bearing a tray laden with food.

'Now,' said he cheerfully, 'may I tempt you to a piece of Betsy's chicken-pie? Despite her shortcomings, she is an excellent cook and you may depend upon it that you will lack for nothing in that way during your stay here.'

Judith experienced the sensation of living through a dream as he helped her to several of the appetizing dishes set before them, talking away as easily as if they were two friends who had chanced to break their journey to partake of a nuncheon at some hostelry. Catching her eyes fixed on him in puzzled question, he put his hand on hers where it lay upon the table and pressed it reassuringly.

'I vow I have more cause than ever to envy Quendon!' he remarked. To her intense mortification, she felt her colour rising.

'I do not understand you, sir. These allusions to the Viscount I find to be most — most —'

'Telling?' he suggested. 'Confess, at all events, that I have put you to the blush!'

'As you would any modest damsel by such indecorous hints!'

she informed him severely. 'I assure you that no understanding exists between Lord Quendon and I — nor, after this episode, is it at all likely that one ever shall.'

'Oh, come!' he quizzed her. 'He is not such a poor creature, is he? If we all play our cards aright and the matter is arranged satisfactorily, no one need know you were ever here.'

'Then where — of course. I stayed with Miss Cartwright.'

'Just so.' He rose and made her a leg, his eyes dancing with mockery, so that her fingers itched to box his ears. 'If you will excuse me I have affairs to attend to, I will send Betsy to you.'

The hours dragged by interminably, Judith's only consolation being that it had come on to rain quite heavily and she had been saved a wetting. The sounds of movement in the yard and a brief glimpse of Timson as he hurried past her window led Judith to suspect that he had brought back Mr Edgecombe's cattle from the George and would, doubtless, return the hired pair when on his way to the Old Hall for, with her gaoler at her shoulder, she had written a short guarded letter to Miss Routledge.

'Be certain that it will be delivered before she has had time to become concerned at your absence,' he comforted her. Judith thanked him politely and resumed her reading of *Mansfield Park*, the one of Miss Austen's novels with which she was not well acquainted and a copy of which she had discovered on a surprisingly well-stocked bookshelf. Mr Edgecombe slipped the note into his pocket then, before she could guess at his intention, he put a hand under her chin and, tilting her face up to him, kissed her lightly upon the lips.

'That to warn you, my lady, that I am a male creature with all such an animal's normal appetites, so do not try my resolution too far!' Then he released her and was gone.

Trembling a little, she set down her book and, reaching for her muff, drew out a handkerchief with which she scrubbed the very touch of his kiss from her mouth. Replacing it, she felt again in the pocket for the cool of the pistol and resolved to keep it close by her. One shot was little enough, in all truth, to protect her, and silently she prayed that her father would be found without loss of time, for it would seem that Mr

Edgecombe was not as indifferent to her as she had supposed. Then she fell to wondering what Miss Routledge would do when she opened her letter and whether she would apply at once for assistance to Netherdene.

*   *   *

As it chanced, Miss Routledge had no need to send for aid for both the Viscount and Lord Penston were with her when Jessop carried in the letter. It was past four o'clock and she was assuring the two gentlemen, who seemed to share her doubts regarding the wisdom of having permitted Miss Hammerton to venture forth in Mr Edgecombe's company, that any moment should see her safely restored to them.

'Delivered by a country fellow, ma'am, who said he was given a shilling to put it into my hand. It is inscribed in miss's writing,' said Jessop pointedly.

Surprised at his putting himself forward in such a manner when visitors were present, she looked at him quickly, a reprimand trembling on the tip of her tongue. Then she perceived the anxiety of his expression and bit back the words.

'Open it, if you please, ma'am,' Lord Penston entreated her.

With a murmured apology she did so and, having read the few lines it contained, uttered a faint cry and turned so pale that Penston felt constrained to support her while Rodney possessed himself of the letter.

'Great Heaven, he has kidnapped her!' he cried.

'What!' burst simultaneously from Penston and Jessop.

'And will hold her until assured that his life is in no danger from Hammerton or any other.'

'I warned the master no good would come of this!' groaned Jessop.

Rodney swung round upon him. 'You know where he is?'

'I believe him to be belowstairs in the cellars, my lord. Leastways, he was an hour ago but he may well have departed.'

'And you would have allowed us — Miss Hammerton and I, to go to London to-morrow in search of him?' Miss Routledge almost wailed.

'The master would have it so, ma'am. He declared that it was best you should be out of the way for a few days while he — he settled accounts, as he put it.'

'Is he alone?' The hesitancy of Rodney's question caused Penston, who had been favoured with his godson's full confidence that morning, to glance at him in sympathetic understanding.

'So far as I am aware, my lord, he is alone.' Jessop had recovered his composure and was clearly resolved to betray nothing that might not be in his master's interest.

'Would you carry that letter to him, Jessop, if you please?' Penston was equally unruffled. 'We will wait here with Miss Routledge.'

'At once, my lord.'

As the butler turned to leave the saloon, the door flew open and, unannounced, in walked Miss Euphrasia Edgecombe. Animated by a most unwonted determination, she faced the battery of stares that greeted her entrance with admirable aplomb.

'I knew that something was amiss!' she pronounced. 'Where is Jasper?'

'Mr Edgecombe has made off with Miss Hammerton,' Lord Penston explained soothingly, and found himself having to remove his arm hastily from the support of Miss Routledge — who, be it confessed stood in no urgent need of it — and employ it for the same purpose in upholding Miss Edgecombe.

'Oh, no!' she moaned, gazing up at him imploringly. 'It cannot be — he would never subject her to insult or — or unmannerly treatment.'

'On the contrary,' ground out Rodney between his teeth, 'he may well subject her to an excess of civility! When did they set out from here?'

'At ten o'clock prompt this morning, my lord,' said Jessop, pausing by the door to weigh up the possible implications of the latest addition to the party, 'and Chilcot had it from Mr Edgecombe's groom that they were to change horses at the George in Bishop's Stortford.'

Miss Routledge suppressed a horrified gasp. 'That is very

likely all a hum to set us on the wrong track. They could be in London now!'

'He cannot easily treat with us from London,' pointed out Lord Penston sensibly, lowering the wilting Euphrasia into a chair while Miss Routledge, thankful for something useful to do, searched for her aromatic vinegar to wave under that damsel's nose. 'No, I am persuaded he will lie hid somewhere locally. But I cannot fully understand why he fancies that Hammerton seeks his life. You, Rodney, are convinced that Edgecombe means you no harm. For my part, I believe he would be quite astray in the head to attempt any mischief, if for no better reason than that suspicion must naturally fall upon him. After all is said, he is still your heir.'

'Until Quendon marries and begets a son.' Euphrasia's small voice drew the attention of all to her somewhat dishevelled figure. An old faded blue merino mantle had been flung on over a muslin round gown, her bonnet was decidedly askew, and she wore one blue glove and carried a brown one. In all, she presented the appearance of a lady distracted half out of her wits. 'Don't you see?' she went on in the same strange, tight little voice. 'Jasper will attempt nothing against Quendon now, hoping that some quirk of Fate will do the business for him. But if Quendon marries and there is a son of the marriage, then the whole aspect could change.'

'You mean he will do all in his power to prevent the marriage?' Penston said slowly. 'If that is so, Miss Hammerton is in greater peril than we knew.'

'No, no!' Euphrasia, waving Judith's letter which Miss Routledge had taken from Jessop and had given her to peruse, was most emphatic. 'Not for her life, that I promise you. Nor, indeed, for her virtue unless he is forced to it.' She turned piteous eyes towards Rodney. 'You see, I know him very well. But this seizure of his daughter will surely incense Mr Hammerton, and whatever motive may be urging him to — to kill Jasper will now be magnified beyond anything.'

Her voice trembled and broke on the last words, and Miss Routledge took her hand and pressed it warmly. 'Have no fear, Miss Edgecombe. Mr Hammerton is not at all the sort of man to lend himself to unbridled passions. I am confident he can be relied upon to keep the line.' She looked across at Rodney, who stood with clenched fists and flushed cheeks, scowling at the floor. 'And so, I am assured, can Lord Quendon.'

'My God, if he lays a finger on her I'll forestall Hammerton in his intention!' The Viscount's outburst was so vehement that Miss Routledge understood she could be at fault in her assessment of his forbearance, but Penston intervened before more was said on that head.

'It is possible, I allow, that his object may be twofold,' he said doubtfully, 'to restrain Hammerton and to discourage any — er, attachment that may be forming between Quendon and Miss Hammerton.'

'That he'll not do!' growled Rodney.

'Shall we join issue to defeat his purpose, Quendon?' Euphrasia surprised them all by asking. 'Whatever shall be the outcome, you to claim Miss Hammerton, while I take Jasper in charge?'

Rodney and Miss Routledge stared at her in amazement but Penston, more conversant with her sentiments than they, merely asked: 'But what of your mother, Miss Edgecombe?'

She shrugged. 'What of her? I shall be twenty-one and my own mistress within the year when, by my father's will, I come into control of my own monies. I can do what I please then. That,' she added pensively, 'is a circumstance of which Jasper is not fully aware.'

'How does it come about that you are here now?' asked Miss Routledge, regarding her with lively curiosity.

'I heard only this afternoon of Jasper's plan to go to Bishop's Stortford and of his calling here to take up Miss Hammerton. I cannot explain why but I immediately became anxious and knew you would be, too, Miss Routledge. Mama is visiting at Saffron Walden so I hastened over at once.'

Jessop re-entered the room at that moment, wearing a most concerned expression. 'Mr Hammerton is not to be found,' he said, 'and has left me a message saying he may not return until late this evening.'

'Then, for God's sake, let us be away and seek out

Edgecombe!' implored Rodney, his concern for Judith betraying him into impatient speech. 'If he did indeed bait his horses at the George, then we may have news of him there.'

'I'll take the gig,' announced Miss Routledge with decision.

'You will do no such thing, not by yourself, not with that wrist!' declared Penston. Miss Routledge was about to protest indignantly at such high-handed dealing when Euphrasia intervened in her quiet voice.

'It would be best, do you not think, to dispense with the grooms? The fewer people know about this adventure the better. I can drive the gig.'

'Quite right,' approved Penston. 'Rodney, you can come up with me or accompany Miss Edgecombe, as you please, but you are in no case as yet to be handling the ribbons.'

'Shall I expect you back to-night, ma'am?' Jessop enquired of Miss Routledge.

'Yes — no! I do not know. It is half-past four already, I cannot imagine it to be likely that we shall return before the morning.' She appealed to Penston. 'What do you think, my lord?'

'Unless we get a clear direction at the George, we must seek out Miss Cartwright,' he said after consideration. 'But she may not be sufficiently settled in to accommodate our entire party. In which case — there must be an inn nearby where we gentlemen can lodge.'

'There is the Greyhound at Spellbrook, my lord,' volunteered Jessop. 'A very respectable house, I am given to understand.'

'Thank you. And Jessop — that letter received from Miss Hammerton called us urgently to Miss Cartwright's where some catastrophe has overtaken her. She was thrown from her horse and sustained injury, perhaps?'

'That won't do for mama,' said Euphrasia. 'Best to say that Miss Cartwright wished you all to dine with her and stay the night, as she is in need of aid and advice, and you have pressed me to be of the party.'

'Miss Cartwright being in need of aid and advice sounds the most unlikely thing,' remarked Penston with the ghost of a smile, 'but, for want of a better, that tale must stand.'

'And I had best go and instruct Sarah to put up a night case,' said Miss Routledge with decision. 'And some attire for you, too, Miss Edgecombe.'

'Euphrasia, if you please,' said that young lady shyly. 'May I come with you, Miss Patience? I must write a few lines for mama and send my groom back with them. I feel — I *know* I must present a very odd appearance, but I left Netherdene in great haste.'

'Of course.' Miss Routledge put an arm around Euphrasia's shoulders and led her away. 'And perhaps we can find you something a little more suitable than that mantle!'

'We will set out in ten minutes, if you please,' Penston called after them.

His tone, while perfectly courteous, caused a little shiver to run up Miss Routledge's spine for, like many capable and self-reliant ladies, she enjoyed being obliged to submit to male domination upon occasion, provided always that the male concerned was one whom she could both trust and respect. In this instance, her anxiety for Judith was so great that she could only be thankful that Penston had taken command of the situation.

Rodney was in like case. The fury he had experienced at the thought of Mr Edgecombe's two-faced dealing with him had, when added to his fears for Judith's safety, rendered him almost incapable of coherent reasoning. Drawing a deep breath, he addressed his godfather:

'And if we do not discover Mr Hammerton to-day?'

'I suspect that Miss Cartwright may be able to provide us with knowledge of his whereabouts.' There was more than a touch of astringency in Penston's voice.

'And my father? Jasper was convinced that he cannot be far away.'

'Yes, Sir Rollo.' Penston, hands clasped beneath his coat-tails, slowly paced the room.

'Surely he must realize that if he — if anyone — if Jasper is killed, then all chance of his proving his innocence is lost?'

'Even were he disposed to tell the truth, such proof cannot rest on Edgecombe's testimony alone. Once it was revealed that he was Sir Rollo's natural son, would it not be the most likely thing that he should be wishful of clearing his father's name?'

'Maybe, were the father not Sir Rollo!'

The distress in the vibrant young voice affected Penston strongly but he went on talking calmly as if unaware of Rodney's anguish of spirit. 'No, what is required here is the mademoiselle's testimony and *that* we are not likely to come by, for she'll not commit herself to clear Sir Rollo.'

'Sir, think of him what you will, but of this one crime he is innocent.'

'There are many others he might answer for!' Never before could Rodney remember seeing his lordship so implacably stern, but further discussion was prohibited by the entrance of Jessop with the information that he had placed a few things in a valise for the gentlemen's convenience, since he apprehended that their return to Netherdene that evening was hardly to be expected.

CHAPTER
TWELVE

TIME had hung heavily upon Miss Hammerton's hands, and the afternoon had been spent in fruitless contemplation of her unfortunate plight.

A careful examination of the parlour in which she was being held prisoner had proved that the single opening vent in the window, which was scarce large enough to allow of the passage of a cat, and the massive oak door, provided the only means of entry. Prompted by hopeful recollections of the secret passage at the Old Hall, she had tapped and pressed on the panelling, but had discovered nothing more rewarding than a clothes closet with several articles of gentlemen's clothing, neatly pressed and put away. As these seemed to be altogether too small to accommodate Mr Edgecombe's robust person and also bore a slightly worn and outmoded air, she concluded that Betsy kept them in tender memory of her nursling as he had been when a boy. The parlour itself provided nothing that might conceivably be used as a weapon. Though a fire was laid in the grate, the day was too mild to allow of its being lit, and no fireirons were to be seen.

'Not even a poker!' sighed Judith wistfully, then her eye fell upon the exceptionally unattractive and solid vase that stood upon the mantelshelf. She lifted it down and weighed it thoughtfully in her hands, then set it, more convenient to need, on a small side-table. Betsy, she was persuaded, would not notice its change of position until she came to clean the room and, in the unlikely event of Mr Edgecombe's doing so, he would surely attribute it to the old woman's having taken it down to dust and forgotten to replace it.

Mr Edgecombe did his captive the honour of dining with her that evening, but neither by word or gesture did he hint at what had taken place at their previous encounter. He was once again the conversable companion that he had shown himself to be for two months past, yet she could not be easy in her mind, although grateful to be able to conceal her misgivings under an assumed air of cheerfulness. More than anything, she longed to ask him if her letter had been delivered to the Old Hall, but her pride forbade her to show any anxiety on so delicate a subject, and he made no mention of it.

She forced herself to make an excellent dinner and maintained an easy flow of conversation as if she had nothing more on her mind than the whims of the weather or the latest turn of fashion. When the very creditable repast was removed, Mr Edgecombe begged her permission to leave her for a time. 'It is my custom to blow a cloud after dinner each evening,' he explained. 'My aunt will not have it that I indulge myself in the dining-room for, she claims, the smoke damages the drapes, so I take myself outside when possible. Would you care for a game of cribbage or piquet later? And at what hour shall I require Betsy to bring in tea?'

Under cover of giving this important question her serious consideration, Judith was thinking furiously. She had no doubt that the receipt of her letter at the Old Hall must have had dramatic effect and that, by now, for it was past seven o'clock, her friends would have followed her progress at least as far as the George, though what misleading rumours Timson had put about there she did not dare to contemplate. In any event, she surmised that they would seek out Miss Cartwright at Fairacre and surely could not be very far away, providing always that the tale of her having been spirited off to London had not gained too much credit with them. A gentle cough from Mr Edgecombe recalled her to a sense of the present.

'I think at half-past nine, if you please,' she said composedly. He bowed, the perfect host, deferring to her every wish.

'Then I shall return with the cards in half an hour or so, and we shall set to.'

When he had left her and she was at leisure to consider her problems, she went over the scheme that was half-forming in her mind. Until the tea-tray had been carried in, she dared not make any attempt to escape. By then, it would be quite dark but

she would be plunged into a strange country with not the least
idea of which way to turn. To arrive at Georgiana's house must be
her object and she had no notion of where that might be. Mr
Edgecombe had made mention of Spellbrook. If she could but
find her way to the Greyhound, then surely she could be directed
to Fairacre from there. A rueful sigh escaped her as she visualized
the arrival on foot at a reputable inn of a somewhat travel-worn
lady, with neither baggage nor attendants to lend her
countenance, and at a late hour of night.

'No, that will never do, my girl,' she mused, and then, 'oh, you
blockhead! The garments in the closet! Clothed in those you
could pass off as a lad in indifferent light!'

It was the work of moments to get the clothes from the closet.
The riding-coat fitted admirably and she quickly decided on that
with buckskins and boots as being preferable to breeches and a
cutaway coat. The boots she discovered to be several sizes too
large but, by wearing two pairs of thick woolen stockings, she
fancied she could overcome that difficulty. Of shirts there was a
good selection but, to her dismay, no neckcloths. This obstacle
was overcome when she unfolded a spotted silk scarf, somewhat
shabby but quite passable.

'The very thing!' she breathed. 'Tied à la Belcher, with this
beaver — faugh! It is thick with dust!'

It was a shade large, too, but by stuffing more stockings into the
crown, it came down no further than her ears and concealed every
vestige of her bright hair. Satisfied, she returned everything neatly
to its former position and was sitting, immersed once more
in *Mansfield Park*, when Mr Edgecombe returned with the
cards.

Quite what she had in mind to do Judith was not very clear,
but certain it was that she had no intention of spending a night
under the same roof as her abductor if such a situation could be
avoided. He might protest that he had no intention of molesting
her but, after the disturbing incident of the afternoon, she
placed little faith in his protestations. She hoped she might not
have to use her pistol upon him, for that would leave her
defenceless against Timson should he return to the cottage that
night.

Her apprehensions were in no way calmed by the appearance of a bottle of wine to which Mr Edgecombe applied himself liberally during their play for, though he gave no indication of being in the least castaway, he had broached one bottle already during his play and Miss Hammerton was forced to exert herself to some degree in order to provide sufficiently stout opposition for so nimble an opponent.

Far from frowning upon his libations, however, she did everything in her power to encourage him to persevere with them, even to the length of accepting a glass or two herself and allowing him to call for another bottle, her design being to keep him entertained until the tea-tray had been brought in, by which time she prayed that the amount of wine he had consumed would have taken effect, and she could the more easily catch him at a disadvantage.

It did occur to her to wonder whether he might not be bolstering up his courage by imbibing so deeply and, once again, she suffered the mortification of having her thoughts read with uncanny accuracy when, watching her over the rim of his glass, he chuckled suddenly.

'Have no fear, ma'am, I am not generally considered to be dangerous until I have finished my third bottle!'

Miss Hammerton replied tranquilly that it depended upon what he meant by dangerous, and the game proceeded without further comment. The key, she observed, he had left in the lock and, indeed, had not troubled to turn it, no doubt considering his presence to be adequate safeguard.

As ever, he gave all the appearance of being perfectly at his ease so that, when she inadvertently dropped a card on the floor and he moved to pick it up, she was quite taken aback when he remained on one knee beside her and, clasping her hand, kissed it with such fervour as to cause her to draw away from him in alarm.

'Do restrain yourself, I beg of you, sir!' she protested lightly, trying to make a jest of the matter. He looked up at her and the glow in his eyes, even if only prompted by the wine he had consumed, was none the less disturbing for that.

'You are too lovely,' he muttered thickly, 'When I look at you I forget all my good resho — resolutions.'

'Allow me to inform you that you are making a great cake of yourself, Mr Edgecombe!' she retorted, endeavouring to rise, but at once his arms were around her, clasping her to him while he still remained upon his knees. 'Oh, you can have no idea how absurd you look!' she taunted him, hoping that ridicule might have more effect than remonstrance upon his somewhat fuddled understanding, but in this she found herself to be vastly mistaken.

'Laugh at me, would you? I'll teach you manners, my girl!'

His sudden anger so startled her that, as he got unsteadily to his feet, she kicked out and thrust herself away from him. Her chair overturned with a crash and Mr Edgecombe, muttering a savage imprecation, staggered back and bent to rub his injured shin. Judith, taking advantage of his momentary inattention, snatched up the heavy vase from the side-table and brought it down with considerable force upon his head.

For an appreciable moment nothing happened then, quite slowly, he fell forward to lie at her feet amid the fragments of china, a slow trickle of blood showing on the collar of his coat. Miss Hammerton, understandably concerned at what she had done, dropped to her knees beside him but could discover no damage other than a small cut at the back of his head, and formed the opinion that his insensibility was as much due to his libations as to the blow she had struck him.

Assured that his life was in no danger, she looked at the clock on the mantelshelf which showed the time to be a few minutes short of half-past nine. Keeping a vigilant eye on Mr Edgecombe's recumbent form, she changed swiftly out of her feminine clothing into the garments she had selected from the closet then, removing from the pocket of her muff the roll of banknotes she had prudently thought to bring with her and the pistol, she tried the door-handle which yielded to her touch. The sound of clattering china warned her that Betsy's arrival was imminent and, possessing herself of the key, she stationed herself behind the door. Presently the old woman bustled along and, thrusting open the door, bore in her tea-tray, whereupon

Judith stepped smartly out of the room and locked the door behind her, being followed by a wail of anguish which momentarily arrested her flight to the outer door.

Once outside, she stood pressed close to the wall of the cottage, the pistol held ready in her hand. The rain had ceased but the sky was overcast and a gusty wind shook the branches of the trees. Then, as Betsy's cries grew more insistent, she darted forward to where she surmised the gate must be. He eyes becoming more accustomed to the dark, she swiftly unlatched it and was presently standing in the lane. Her plans had not progressed as far as this point and she hesitated, wondering which way she should turn. Muffled shouts and thumps emanating from the cottage quickly made up her mind for her and, recalling that, on their way up the narrow track that morning, she and Mr Edgecombe had passed no habitation of any kind since leaving the turnpike road, she resolved to direct her steps in the opposite direction. To her surprise, she found she was still clutching the door-key and, pausing only to throw it as hard and as high as was in her power over the hedge on the farther side of the lane, she set out at a brisk pace to put as much distance between herself and the cottage as was possible.

Desperately, she pressed on, half-running, half-walking, but she had not traversed fifty yards when her over-large boots finally betrayed her and she fell headlong, rolling over and ending up, breathless, in the thick grass beneath the hedge. It was then she heard a sound that sent her wildly-beating heart into her hampering boots, that of hoofbeats thudding along the lane and, a moment later, a horseman passed her at a smart trot.

Blessing her good fortune at having been thrown down out of his sight, she lay unmoving for a moment, not fully comprehending that he was proceeding in the direction from which she had come and could, therefore, not be on the look for her. As soon as her agitated brain had grasped this fact she scrambled to her feet, debating how best to turn this unexpected development to her advantage. It was plain that she was not going to get very far afoot, therefore she must, by some means, obtain a mount. The horseman most likely was Timson, coming to rejoin his master; even if it were not he no one would be likely to ride past the cottage, from whence issued a veritable uproar of noise, without at least reining in to enquire the cause. The far-off sound of tinkling glass seemed to augur that Betsy had, very sensibly, left off thumping on the door and had applied herself to breaking the window. With Timson to help her and the return to sensibility of Mr Edgecombe, it would be no time before a search was mounted so she had better make use of the few minutes of freedom left to her.

Even as she was turning over the possibilities in her mind, her feet were directing her back to the cottage where she found, to her relief, that Timson had tethered his horse to the gate-post while he ran to render what help he could to Betsy. That animal started and stamped nervously as she approached but obeyed readily enough when she took hold of the bridle and led him into the lane. Putting a foot in the stirrup, she swung herself into the saddle, praying that the creature would submit to her handling.

He proved to be docile enough and, once around a bend in the lane and out of sight of the cottage, she urged him to any easy canter. The clouds were clearing away and a thin moon supplied a pale, diffused light for which she was grateful when they came to where a wider road cut across their small track. Having no notion of which way she ought to go, she gave the horse his head but, observing the confident manner in which he took the new road, she experienced a sudden qualm lest he should be heading for his stable. The reflection caused her no little apprehension for, once arrived there, questions would surely be asked as to how she had come by the animal. Then they were joining the turnpike road and, finding that he clearly favoured turning to the left along it, she judged it prudent to force him to go in the opposite direction. This, he made very plain, he had no wish to do, and the next few minutes were occupied in asserting her authority over him after which they went on in a more amicable fashion, if less willingly than before.

Taking advantage of the better road and the moonlight, they were making good progress when she perceived the lights of a carriage ahead of her.

'Now what to do?' she ruminated. 'Overtake them and seek a

direction, or lag behind? And if I do ride up to them do I not risk being taken for a footpad and shot at by an over-zealous groom? And if I lag behind, there is no knowing what may overtake me!'

She checked her steed down to a trot while she deliberated upon a choice. The vehicle in front appeared to be going ever more slowly and she soon must be obliged to draw level or be content to proceed at a walk. In the event of a pursuit, which she had no doubt was already in course, she dared not risk too slow a progress and, as the carriage disappeared round a bend of the road, she urged her horse forward and all but dashed head-on into the back of the vehicle where it was drawn up across the road.

A faint cry escaped her as she perceived a figure standing beside it, the moonlight glinting off the barrels of the pistol held steadily pointed in her direction.

'Now,' said a crisply commanding voice, 'let us look at you, my good fellow, and discover your intent.'

'Your pardon, sir,' gasped Judith in as manly a voice as she could muster, 'but I have lost my direction and would be grateful if you could set me right.'

The man holding the pistol did not waver nor was the gentleman's voice any more cordial when he made reply. 'And where had you in mind?' he enquired.

'I would be obliged, sir, if you could direct me to Sir Humphrey Cartwright's residence,' she said nervously.

At that, he did lower his weapon and there was an appreciable pause before he replied. 'Fairacre, you mean? What is your business with Sir Humphrey?'

Miss Hammerton was strongly tempted to require him to mind his own affairs but his still holding the pistol put her at a considerable disadvantage. 'I — it is Miss Cartwright that I wish to see, sir,' she got out at last.

'Oh, it is, is it?' The gentleman sounded alarmingly grim. 'And what circumstance brings you to visit Miss Cartwright at this hour of night?' Then, as she made no answer, he rapped out sharply: 'Get down off your horse and come here!' Feeling more than a trifle uneasy, she was obliged to obey this peremptory command for behind her challenger she discerned another figure, presumably that of his groom, standing to the horses' heads. 'So,' went on the gentleman, looking her up and down, 'you have an assignment with Miss Cartwright, have you?'

His tone was now that of amused raillery and she was more than ever puzzled by his attitude, but it seemed to her that she had better hold to her role of country stripling and answered him as bravely as she could.

'I have not that good fortune, sir. I — I but carry a message for her.'

'I see. A go-between for some other? His name? Answer me, puppy!' As Judith stood, tongue-tied, unable to decide what she should say, he called over his shoulder at his groom. 'Hand me the whip, John!' Then, thrusting the pistol into his coat pocket, he reached out and seized her by the collar. 'Your choice, my lad. I'll have the truth from you or you will have the seat of your breeches dusted — which is it to be?'

Miss Hammerton came to an instant decision. 'If you please, sir, I am not a lad, I am a girl!' she gasped. 'And one in great trouble. I was going to — to Georgy to seek aid.'

'Good God!' said he, releasing her at once and stepping back.

'I was kidnapped, you see, and I escaped and — and they may be following me now, so I must find shelter,' burst out Judith, the words tumbling over themselves in her anxiety to make her predicament clear to him.

'Most understandable,' agreed the gentleman politely. 'Who — er, who kidnapped you?'

'Mr Edgecombe. He — I was going to visit Georgy — Miss Cartwright and he offered to escort me there. Then — then he made an excuse to call upon an old servant of his and, once there, made me his prisoner.'

'Now why should he do that?' wondered her interlocutor mildly. 'Did he wish to force marriage upon you or were his intentions less honourable?'

'Less honourable, I assure you!' Judith's spirits were reviving and with them a certain indignation at being interrogated in such a style. 'He wished to hold me as surety for my father's conduct.'

'Your father? May I ask his name, young lady?'

'Hammerton, Mr George Hammerton.'

At that, to her astonishment, the gentleman gave a great shout of laughter as if at some prime jest. 'So you are George Hammerton's daughter! Well met, Miss — Judith, is it not?'

'Y-yes, it is,' stammered Judith, much taken aback and not a little annoyed at his obvious amusement. 'But who you may be, sir —'

She got no further because he had turned to his groom and was instructing him to take charge of her horse. 'If you will be so kind, ma'am, as to mount into my phaeton, I myself will escort you to Miss Cartwright.' Judith, who was in no mood to be kidnapped twice in a day, hesitated to accept this handsome offer until, still laughing, he swept off his beaver and made her an elegant bow. 'Let me assure you, ma'am, your servant to command!'

Perceiving that he was a man of certain age and one, moreover of good address and undoubted breeding, she allowed him to stand her up into the phaeton. 'You shall tell me the whole while we resume our journey,' he said, gathering the reins into his hands. 'How did you escape from Mr — what did you say his name was?'

'I broke a vase over his head,' she informed him coldly. 'And I fail to see, sir, why my unhappy situation should occasion such levity on your part!'

'Crude but effective,' he commented, taking not the least notice of her reproof. 'I presume you had no other weapon?'

'I have a pistol, but I needed that in case Timson followed me.'

'And who is Timson?' he enquired as he turned his pair as neatly as one could wish and set them on their way, his groom following behind on Judith's horse. Despite her resentment at his unfeeling attitude, he soon obtained all the details of her abduction and, at the end of the recital, remarked thoughtfully: 'But why should your father wish to shoot this fellow Edgecombe? It don't make sense to me — though, of course, I quite understand why he should wish to shoot him *now!*' he added hastily.

'I think sir, you had best ask my father that.'

'I will,' he promised her.

'You know him well, sir?'

'Well enough,' he replied, 'and shall probably know him a deal better when —' He glanced at her and, clearly changing his mind about what he was going to say, went on quickly, 'when we are both settled in these parts.'

She looked at him in surprise. 'I had thought you to be an established resident, sir. You — you seem so sure of your direction and — and your knowledge of my father and Miss Cartwright —'

'Is not at all to be wondered at,' he assured her. 'Shall not a man know the way to his own house and be acquainted with his own daughter?'

'His own house — his daughter — then you are —'

'Sir Humphrey Cartwright, ma'am, arrived in England somewhat unexpectedly. What Georgy's going to say I cannot imagine, but we shall soon know for here we are at Fairacre!'

CHAPTER
THIRTEEN

As Sir Humphrey spoke, the phaeton turned in at a pair of fine iron gates set invitingly open and proceeded up a short, wide drive to a substantial and well-situated house. Fairacre's handsome proportions were the easier to assess by reason of the fact that every window was ablaze with light, while a curricle stood ready, awaiting its passengers, by the short flight of steps leading to the front door.

'Georgy is entertaining, I dare say,' concluded her parent, reining in with a flourish, while the groom standing by the curricle team turned to stare in some astonishment, his eyes widening to saucers as they perceived his master. 'Hey, Whitlock!' called Sir Humphrey genially. 'What's to do here? Must be a rout party at least to account for so prodigal a display of candles!'

The groom's reply was lost in the opening of the front door and the emergence of several persons talking together animatedly.

'Why, it is Lord Penston and — and Lord Quendon!' cried Judith, rising to her feet. 'And — Miss Patience!' This last name, uttered in a small shriek, drew the attention of all.

'Judith!' responded Miss Routledge, hurrying down the steps to greet her charge, who sprang from the phaeton unaided, and ran to embrace her warmly. No sooner had this touching reunion been effected than the Viscount and Lord Penston joined them, both exclaiming in delighted relief at sight of Miss Hammerton. 'But,' went on Miss Routledge in some concern, 'what is this? Why are you dressed in this fashion?'

Judith, acutely aware of her masculine attire and Rodney's ardent gaze, blushed vividly but was saved the trouble of replying by a cry of 'Papa!' from the doorway as Miss Cartwright propelled herself past them and into Sir Humphrey's welcoming arms. 'I had no expectation of seeing you for *weeks!* But where is mama?'

'Refused at the last fence,' reported Sir Humphrey lugubriously. 'We were set, all right and tight, to embark. Lovely day, brisk breeze, we would have completed the passage in fast time, but she's no sailor, it appears, cannot stomach even the smallest swell. It don't signify, though. I'll have to go back in a few weeks and, if you will support me, we will essay it again. Can always dangle the carrot of a wedding under her nose — what? Oh, yes of course! Humph!' He cleared his throat noisily as his daughter gave him an admonishing pinch.

'We will discuss that plan of action later,' said Georgiana, dismissing the subject as if it was of no account. 'What is of the first importance is to discover just what has befallen our dear Judith and how she came to be in your company.'

'Quite simple,' explained her parent. 'Picked her up on the road, running away from some fellow.'

'And I would have been quite in the basket if he had not, I assure you,' said Judith, allowing herself to be led into the house, Rodney and Miss Routledge on either side of her.

'Yes, well, not at all the thing for a young female to be jauntering about unescorted — and in that rig, too!' declared Sir Humphrey in so condemnatory a manner that Judith turned upon him indignantly.

'How can you say so, sir, when you know to what extremities I was forced! I — I was obliged to adopt male costume.'

'And very becoming it is!' he nodded, twinkling at her impishly. 'Evening, Nairn — Quendon, I should say. Had you not better present me to your other friends, Georgy?'

Miss Cartwright, who had led the party through the hall into a finely-proportioned saloon, was about to obey her father's behest, when they were joined by Miss Edgecombe, whose laboured breathing proclaimed her to be under the influence of some strong emotion.

'Miss Hammerton! I knew you must be perfectly safe. 'Twas only a frolic on Jasper's part, was it not?'

Judith's eyes narrowed thoughtfully as she looked into

Euphrasia's anxious ones. 'Not a frolic to my taste, I can assure you,' she replied levelly. Then Rodney was begging Judith to recount her experiences and Georgiana was making her father known to Miss Routledge and Lord Penston, so that small notice was taken of Miss Edgecombe's concern for her cousin and his intentions.

When Judith's tale was told and everyone had expressed their admiration for her resourceful conduct, Euphrasia ventured to enquire if Mr Edgecombe was gravely hurt.

'Depend upon it, he has suffered nothing worse than a sore head,' Judith assured her.

'It will be my pleasure to improve on that discomfort when next I meet him,' muttered Rodney low in her ear. Judith glanced at him quickly. She had been careful to slide over certain aspects of Mr Edgecombe's behaviour but, as she saw the anger flaring in the Viscount's eyes, she realized that he had not been wholly deceived and, in an attempt to divert him, made light of the situation.

'He fancies himself to be in some danger from my father,' she said, accepting with gratitude the glass of wine Georgiana pressed upon her. 'Which was his given reason for holding me captive until papa might be brought to another way of thinking. He was of the opinion that the news of my abduction would reach my father's ears very speedily through some confidant at the Old Hall.'

'That would be Jessop,' Miss Routledge informed her, 'but even he is in ignorance of Mr Hammerton's whereabouts.'

'He'll turn up once he gets wind of my arrival,' remarked Sir Humphrey, sipping his wine appreciatively. 'Damned good burgundy this, Georgy, could not have chosen better myself.'

'Most likely you could not,' agreed his daughter, 'since you did choose it yourself! It is the last that Mr Tullett has been keeping safe for you and arrived only t'other day from Goodge Street.'

'What? Sowerby's that was?' Lord Penston, who had also been savouring the burgundy with approval, was roused to interest and, at once, the two gentlemen became absorbed in a discussion regarding the relative merits of this vintage or that.

While Miss Cartwright's attention appeared greatly taken with watching the Viscount and Miss Hammerton talking quietly together, Miss Routledge was recalled to a proper sense of her duties by observing how excessively well Judith's masculine attire became her trim figure.

'Come, my dear,' she said firmly. 'I have a change of clothing for you upstairs. Euphrasia,' she added, addressing the downcast Miss Edgecombe, 'I believe Judith's valise is in your room. May we make ourselves free of it?'

Miss Edgecombe gave her willing approval and Miss Routledge, drawing her arm through Judith's, led her away. Rodney's attentive gaze followed them until Miss Cartwright's amused voice beside him roused him from his reverie.

'What a courageous girl she is, to be sure! I declare I could almost feel sympathy for Mr Edgecombe.'

'It is far otherwise with me.' Rodney's terse reply caused her to raise an eyebrow in half-humorous question.

'You were not thinking of calling him to account, were you?'

The Viscount, a trifle on his high ropes at this intrusion into his private intentions, made sharp response. 'A sound horse-whipping should cool his ardour!' he rapped out.

She looked him up and down as a prospective buyer might when judging the points of a likely young colt. 'You're not up to his weight,' she pronounced. 'Best leave it to her father. After all, he has the right.'

'I believe him to have a somewhat biased opinion of Edgecombe's villainy. He could be mistaken.'

'So?' Her eyes widened in surprise. 'You do not consider your cousin Jasper to be a complete sharp?'

'He has certain reason on his side,' replied Rodney evasively.

'But, like many men, is "undone by not going deep enough in roguery"!' she quoted. 'Yet I wonder if Judith has told us all the story? I have no doubt, however, that Miss Patience will have the whole from her.'

This prediction was being fulfilled at that very moment in Miss Edgecombe's bedchamber abovestairs.

'While you are changing out of those very dashing garments,' said Miss Routledge, seating herself upon the bed, 'tell me precisely what passed between you and Mr Edgecombe that obliged you to shatter a vase over his head.'

'I could have shot him, you know,' pointed out Judith mildly, removing her riding-coat. 'Had I not worn these breeches I could never have ridden astride. Oooh!' She rubbed her thighs ruefully. 'I shall suffer for it to-morrow!'

'Judith,' said Miss Routledge in the tone of one who intends to have a straight answer has she to wait until Doomsday for it, 'did he molest you?'

'Well, he kissed me once.' Miss Hammerton seemed to be considering if such action came under the heading of being molested. 'And he was becoming quite drunk,' she added, as if summoning up more evidence to justify her behaviour.

'So that you feared he might press further attentions upon you?' pursued Miss Routledge relentlessly.

'I did not relish the prospect of being in the same house with him for a night.' Miss Hammerton's attention was fully engaged in drawing off her heavy boots and several pairs of stockings.

'Of course the very thought offends every sense of propriety,' agreed Miss Routledge.

'Gentlemen are so unpredictable.' Judith cast the last stocking on the bed and began to unbutton her shirt. 'He did offer to marry me.'

'Handsome of him in the circumstances!' Miss Routledge's voice was heavy with sarcasm.

'And added that if I was not rescued soon I would have no choice but to consent to the match.'

'Your reputation being quite irretrievably ruined,' assented Miss Routledge drily, getting up to assist Miss Hammerton out of her breeches and shirt and into an elegant gown of soft green sarcenet, worn over a cream satin petticoat. 'What a good thing I thought to bring this with me. You declined his offer, of course?'

'Of course. Should I have been obliged to accept if he had?'

'If he had what? Do you prefer the gold ribbons to the silver?'

'Yes, I think so. Ravished me, I mean.'

Miss Routledge, who was experiencing a profound sense of relief that nothing of a disastrous nature appeared to have overtaken her charge, drew a deep breath. ''Pon my soul, Judith,' she said wrathfully, 'you treat of the matter very lightly!'

'I always had my pistol, you know. If I had failed to use it in time to — to prevent him, then I could have turned it upon myself afterwards.'

The slight quaver in the girl's steady voice was sufficient rebuke to her companion. 'Forgive me, my dear, I should have known better than that,' she said gently.

For a moment Judith's composure deserted her and she pressed her hands to her cheeks. 'Let us not make too great a thing about this,' she pleaded, 'lest — anyone should feel obliged to defend my honour to the danger of his own life. The very thought of — oh, dear Miss Patience! He would never have looked at me after that, would he?'

Miss Routledge did not need to be told who 'he' was. 'As you yourself have said, gentlemen are unpredictable!' she quizzed, smiling. 'But, depend upon it, he is completely bewitched by you and, I feel sure, only awaits your father's return to make his offer.' She picked up the discarded riding-coat and was about to put it away when her hand struck something hard in a pocket. 'Great Heavens! Your pistol!'

Judith took it from her. 'I had forgot — it is primed, too. I had best attend to that at once.'

'If you please.' Miss Routledge was going through the other pockets. 'Did you carry any other lethal weapons upon your person? What is this that crackles in the lining — oh, it is an inner pocket, almost a secret one so neatly is it hidden away.' She drew out a sheet of paper folded small and opened it.

'That is nothing of mine.' Judith was giving her full attention to her pistol but her head came up sharply when Miss Routledge read out:

'"Three bolts of French cambric, Valenciennes and Chantilly lace" — I cannot make out the amount — "silver tablewear fashioned by Odiot, twelve kegs of brandy —" Why, what is all this?'

Judith put down the pistol and held out her hand for the

paper. 'It appears to me remarkably like a free-trader's list of cargoes,' she said, perusing it carefully. 'The ink has faded and there are stains like — salt-water, perhaps?'

They looked at each other in consternation. 'It is quite old,' said Miss Routledge at last in the tone of one who knows her remark may not be helpful but has to be said.

'Yes, doubtless thrust away in the pocket of an outgrown coat and forgotten.' Judith folded up the list and tapped it thoughtfully against her thumbnail. 'So that is the connection and the reason for much that has perplexed me.'

Miss Routledge sat down again, feeling as if her knees might not support her for very much longer if she did not. 'Mr Edgecombe is a free-trader?'

'Is — or was. My father also, I believe, and doubtless, Sir Rollo Nairn. You don't look overly surprised, Miss Patience.'

'I confess to having suspected that Mr Hammerton had dealings with the free-traders. His generous gifts of French lace and perfume at a time when none could be had, his superb wines and brandy — well, I may not be awake upon every suit, but even I guessed there must be a screw loose somewhere.'

'More than just dealings, I fancy.' Judith's brow was furrowed in thought. 'I collect my father and Mr Edgecombe were together in the business and Sir Rollo hand-in-glove with them. But now they have fallen out. I wonder why?'

Further speculation on this absorbing topic was arrested by a timid tap on the door and Miss Edgecombe's voice asking if she might be admitted. The two ladies exchanged a swift glance.

'She may assist us here,' said Judith, then raising her voice, called out: 'Yes, please come in.'

Miss Edgecombe appeared to have recovered her spirits and spoke in a tolerably composed manner. 'It is only to ask if you would have an objection to sharing this room with me to-night, Miss Hammerton? Sir Humphrey declares that for the two gentlemen to be seeking a lodging at the Greyhound would offend his sense of hospitality, but the thing is that not all the bedchambers have been set in order to receive guests as yet and, though Miss Cartwright is one who is always up to everything, even she cannot perform miracles. Oh!' She clapped her hands together in unaffected delight. 'What a becoming gown! And with those bunches of gold ribbon to match your hair I declare the effect to be quite ravishing!'

Her use of the adjective brought involuntary smiles to her listeners' lips and impulsively, Judith held out a welcoming hand. 'Of course, I have no objection — indeed, I seem to have possessed myself of your room. Do please join us, Euphrasia — I may call you that?'

Miss Edgecombe blushed in gratification. 'Oh, yes, if you please. It is much more comfortable than an excess of formality, is it not?'

'Does this, I wonder, mean anything to you?' said Judith in a deceptively casual tone, holding out the sheet of paper. 'We found it in the coat I was wearing, presumably an old one of Mr Edgecombe's.'

No sooner had Euphrasia commenced to read the listed items than every vestige of colour left her cheeks, her eyes dilated in horror and her hand shook so that the paper rustled as if in a strong breeze. 'I — how could he keep such evidence! The foolish boy!'

Miss Hammerton, who considered Mr Edgecombe to be many things but certainly not foolish, guided the trembling girl to a chair. 'You knew of this — traffic of his?'

'How could I not?' Euphrasia raised tear-drenched eyes to the beautiful, sympathetic face bending over her. 'He — he was forever giving me little gifts and, being careless in my company, often let slip things that could have had but one interpretation. He was like a brother to me, you understand, and I — I gave him that loyalty.'

'But now your feeling for him exceeds simple loyalty, does it not?'

'Yes,' confessed Euphrasia, hanging her head. 'I love him deeply, but to him I am still just the young cousin he has always cherished a little, bullied a little, watched over and —' She paused, a half-smile trembling through her tears.

'And in the process, taken in great affection?' suggested Miss Routledge.

'Oh, he has a kindness for me and, maybe, when he finds there is no hope of attaching an heiress like Miss — Judith, and that my expectations are greater than he knew, he may offer for me. My mother will not care for it above half, but what has that to say to anything? I do not take with gentlemen, having neither countenance nor accomplishments, and Jasper, being an Edgecombe, is not wholly ineligible.'

Her affecting humility and her obvious devotion to her disreputable cousin so touched Judith that she was moved to embrace the girl.

'I think you will be the very best possible wife for him,' she said, 'for you know all his faults and love him in spite of them. But to revert to this business of the smuggling, does it still continue?'

'I believe so, though since —' She looked at Judith in some distress, unwilling to continue.

'Since my father went away?'

Euphrasia sighed in relief. 'I do not fully understand how it all began, but Jasper worked for Mr Hammerton in his counting-house in London for a time. Then he came back to the Old Hall where his parents lived. His father's understanding was never great, in fact by that time he was quite out of his mind, and his mother was a kindly enough but bird-brained creature who would notice nothing that went on under her nose, so —'

'So the cellars of the Old Hall were put to good use,' Judith concluded for her. 'And you think they still are being so employed?'

Euphrasia nodded. 'Jasper was used to call there at least once a week. He pretended it to be an affection for the old house, but I was not deceived. He was forced to go to Thaxted with his mother when her sister's husband died and she begged them to make their home with her, and by the time Mrs Edgecombe had passed away your father had bought the Old Hall. I wondered what he would do when you came to live there.'

'He continued to make his weekly visits,' said Judith with a rueful chuckle. 'And I thought they were occasioned by a partiality for my company!'

'This is all very well,' said Miss Routledge, who had been

listening in silence for some minutes, 'but why does Mr Hammerton now wish to shoot Mr Edgecombe?'

At this point Miss Cartwright's voice was heard outside the door, summoning them downstairs. 'For,' she explained, 'the gentlemen are to remain with us to-night and declare they are in sore need of feminine company.'

It was a merry enough party that gathered in the saloon, combining as it did a celebration for Judith's safe return with a welcome home for Sir Humphrey. Only two people seemed a shade out of touch with the light-hearted mood of the evening, Miss Edgecombe and, less understandably, Miss Cartwright. Judith could not but observe how Georgiana's eyes often sought the clock and, as the hands moved around to midnight, how her ebullient spirits seemed to flag.

The wind had died away and the air had become so warm and still that the French windows had been thrown wide. Judith stepped outside to look up at the clear sky with its young crescent moon, and wondered aloud at the pleasing change in the weather.

'Yes,' said Rodney's voice at her elbow. 'Sir Humphrey could have no excuse for mistaking you for a lad on so fair a night.' As she turned to him, he took her hands and kissed them and held them pressed against his breast. 'Miss Hammerton — Judith, I have to say it though I vowed I would not until I had spoken to your father, but this evening the fear that I might have lost you has proved too much for my resolution.' He loosed one hand to touch a curling tendril of her hair. 'I have wanted you for my wife, I believe, from the first moment that ever I saw you but had small hope you would be unwed when I returned to England.'

'Five years faithful, my lord?' she teased him archly, but her heart was beating as if to choke her as he bent his head to hers. A soft scuffle in the undergrowth nearby caused her to start and move into his willing embrace. 'W-what was that?' she whispered nervously.

'A mouse?' He laughed softly. 'Can you be frightened after all, my brave love? If so, thank God for it! Fearless Amazons are all very well but not for every occasion!'

A deep voice broke in on their preoccupation. 'Well,' it said, 'I come to rescue her from the attentions of one gentleman and find her in the embrace of another! You move too fast, my girl!'

'Father!' gasped Judith, detaching herself from Rodney's arms and casting herself upon her parent. 'Father! Father!'

'Hey, steady, lass!'. Mr Hammerton admonished her kindly. 'Reserve a little affection for his lordship, he seems to think well of it!'

But the Viscount paid no heed to this quip for he was staring at another figure, overshadowed by Mr Hammerton's great bulk, standing motionless with hat pulled over his brow. As the unknown raised his head to look towards the window a shaft of candlelight fell fleetingly across his face, and Rodney was moved to repeat Judith's cry, but in a broken whisper: 'Father!'

A low chuckle broke from the other. 'Grieved to have to inform you, Quendon, no such thing!' said Mr Jasper Edgecombe, stepping forward. 'I am flattered, of course, more particularly as our revered parent is not longer in a position to cause unease to either of us. Miss Hammerton, your most obedient. I am sorry you felt obliged to take leave of me in so — shattering a manner!'

'Enough of that, Edgecombe!' said Mr Hammerton harshly. 'Did he lay finger on you, Judith?'

'Nothing to signify, I promise you,' she said quickly.

'Edgecombe, you'll answer to me for this!' At the rasp of anger in Rodney's voice, Judith's hands were on his shoulders, restraining him.

'No, no, he has answered to me already!' she whispered, rising on tip-toe to kiss his cheek.

'Let me tell you, my girl, this behaviour is not at all the thing!' said her father severely. 'And if you are deluding yourself into thinking that Quendon will be offering for you after such a display of forwardness, you'll find you have much mistaken the matter.'

Rodney, quite unable to maintain any semblance of indignation with so tender an armful in his grasp, was obliged to laugh. 'Oh, no, she has not, sir! And if I may discuss the matter with you —'

'To-morrow,' agreed Mr Hammerton, patting his arm. 'But it grows late and there are still things which must be told. Shall we go in?'

CHAPTER
FOURTEEN

FROM inside the room Miss Routledge could just discern the figures of Miss Hammerton and the Viscount on the terrace, and debated to herself whether she ought not to summon Judith to come in. Then she caught Lord Penston's eye and found him laughing at her.

'May not a gentleman propose to a lady without being harried by Madame Propriety?' he breathed.

'You think he is — doing that?'

'I consider it to be most likely!' he assured her, the solemnity of his tone belied by his amused expression, for he had correctly assessed the powerful stimulus that Judith's safe return had given to Rodney's affections. Miss Routledge glanced again towards the window and her eyes narrowed in concentration.

'But — surely they are not alone? There are other persons there!'

'What?' He sprang to his feet and she with him, while the others in the room looked towards them in question.

'It's — it *is*!' announced Miss Routledge in what she quite understood to be the most idiotish way, as Judith entered the room, followed by Mr Hammerton, Rodney, and Mr Edgecombe.

'Good-evening, Miss Routledge,' said the large gentleman, making her a civil bow. 'I may say that I am not a little concerned to find, upon my return after so long an absence, my daughter clasped in the arms —'

'Hush, father, please!' begged Judith, her cheeks aflame.

'Allowing them a little license, were you, ma'am?'

But Mr Hammerton was not permitted to enlarge upon this diverting theme for, with a rustle of silken skirts, a suddenly radiant Georgiana had come to greet him and he bent to kiss her out-stretched hand with every appearance of delight.

Then Miss Edgecombe, too, came to life. 'Jasper, your poor face! What has befallen you?' she wailed.

This artless enquiry drew the attention of all to Mr Edgecombe's countenance, which indeed presented a sorry appearance. One eye was partly closed and richly discoloured, while a swollen underlip gave further evidence of violence done to his person.

'I — ah, ran into something!' he explained lamely, 'Now, Euphrasia, don't fly into the boughs, there's a good girl!'

'Ran into something, indeed!' she raged. 'It was — it was you, wasn't it?' she accused Mr Hammerton. 'Why don't you pick on someone of your own size?'

'I try, ma'am, but 'tis difficult to find such great gawks as me,' he replied meekly, allowing his Yorkshire burr to get the better of him.

'I th-thought you were g-going to shoot him, anyway,' she quavered.

'I was, ma'am, but then I fancied first giving him a little something on account of running off with my Judith.'

'Oh, father, and I had hit him with the vase!' protested Judith.

'Yes, but he didn't tell me that until afterwards.'

'Small chance I had of telling you anything!' complained Mr Edgecombe, who felt he was being made to look ridiculous and resented it.

'Anyway, I do not intend to shoot him now, ma'am,' Mr Hammerton assured Miss Edgecombe.

She sniffed. 'Very magnanimous of you, to be sure! Come and sit down, Jasper, you don't look at all the thing.'

Sir Humphrey, who had been watching this little scene with considerable interest, now advanced to greet Mr Hammerton.

'Glad to see you, George. I hope all this makes sense to you for I can tell you it don't to me.'

Mr Hammerton looked from him to Rodney. 'You haven't spoken to his lordship?'

Sir Humphrey shook his head. 'Your place to do that, George.'

Mr Hammerton squared his great shoulders and addressed

himself to Rodney. 'I have the misfortune to have to inform you, my lord, that you are in very truth the Viscount Quendon. Your father is — no more.'

A respectable silence fell over the company, but it was remarkable that no one felt disposed to offer condolences to the Viscount on the loss of his parent.

'Was it because of —?' Rodney glanced significantly towards Mr Edgecombe, but that gentleman hastily denied the accusation.

'None of my doing, I promise you. No, he made a good recovery from that, but Nature herself struck him down.'

''Twas a cancerous tumour,' explained Mr Hammerton. 'He was in very indifferent health when we sailed from Jamaica, but he would come. Seemed to be urged on by a spirit of — of —' He searched for a word and Mr Edgecombe supplied it.

'Revenge,' he said simply. 'If it cost him his life, he was bent on giving me my own again.'

'I yielded to his importunities,' continued Mr Hammerton, 'for there was little in the way of good medical care to be had in Kingston. I hoped, if I could get him to Lisbon, to engage Sir Humphrey's interest on his behalf, and somehow arrange for him to come to England where he might consult a physician of the eminence of Sir Henry Halford or, if needs be, a surgeon like Brandish or Nooth. But it was not to be. He only survived the voyage by one day. I left the conduct of the obsequies to Sir Humphrey and, acting upon Sir Rollo's last requests to me, set out at once for England.'

'And those requests were?' Lord Penston, who had been a silent spectator for all of this exchange, now thought it proper to take a part in it since Rodney clearly had to be given a little time to absorb the fact of his father's death.

'You'll be Lord Penston, I take it, sir?' Mr Hammerton looked at him closely. 'Aye, Sir Rollo spoke to me of you, and not with any great affection.'

'The aversion was mutual,' returned Penston curtly. 'We had our reasons.'

'Aye, two of 'em. But we'll not come to cuffs on that head, my lord. You were not the object of Sir Rollo's design.' He looked at

Mr Edgecombe, sitting comfortably on the sofa, with Euphrasia by his side. 'It was his natural son whose life he wished me to put a period to, lest he should do a like service for Quendon. Oh, mistake me not,' he said apologetically to Rodney, 'I doubt the reason for such conisderation was an excess of affection for you. It was rather a determination that Mr Jasper Edgecombe should never have the chance to call himself Viscount Quendon.'

'Did you say his — his natural son?' interpolated Miss Routledge in a rather dazed fashion, feeling for a chair, which Lord Penston promptly supplied. Rodney was about to protest at this disclosure by Mr Hammerton when it occured to him that, apart from Miss Routledge, no one in the room appeared to evince the least astonishment at so curious a revelation. To be sure, Mr Edgecombe himself looked a trifle distressed, but his concern appeared to be all for Euphrasia.

'I had hoped to tell you in my own time,' he said, directing a wrathful glare at Mr Hammerton. She smiled at him.

'I have known about that for years,' she informed him. 'I overheard papa and your grandfather discussing your future — oh, long ago, when I was quite a small girl. I did not know what it all meant then, but I felt it was something one should not talk about, so I never made mention of it to anyone.'

'Lady Quendon does not know?'

'Unless papa told her, and that I doubt.'

For answer, he picked up her hand and pressed it to his swollen mouth. 'Thank you, m'dear,' he muttered rather huskily.

'But,' said Miss Routledge pursuing her point with determination, 'Sir Rollo would surely not wish Mr Hammerton to shoot his — his son? No man could be so unnatural a parent.'

'That is something we need not go into here.' Rodney's tone of quiet authority took several persons by surprise, but Mr Hammerton nodded his approval.

'As you say, my lord. It is, after all, a private matter.'

'Since you and I, sire, are to discuss another private matter in the morning,' Rodney drew Judith's arm through his as he spoke, 'would you be so good as to refrain from calling me "my lord"?'

Mr Hammerton grinned disarmingly. 'Eh, but you haven't had my yea or nay on that yet, have you, lad?'

'I'd prefer your blessing, of course, sir.'

'But you'd make do without it? Well, I think none the worse of you for that! I am sorry I shot you, by the way.'

'Oh, it was you, was it?' Rodney looked at him in the liveliest astonishment. 'You damned nearly killed me!'

'I thought you were Jasper, y'see. And only having heard one side of the story — Sir Rollo's — I was hell-bent on terminating his existence.'

'I must commiserate with you on your choice of future father-in-law, Quendon,' drawled Mr Edgecombe. 'Devil of a single-minded fellow — though, I allow, open to reason.'

'I gave you the benefit of the doubt, any road!' snapped Mr Hammerton, his Yorkshire origins becoming more than ever apparent.

'Did you?' mused Mr Edgecombe, stroking his painful face tenderly. 'Then Heaven help me if ever you take me in dislike! By the way, how did you discover me?'

'When I got back to the Old Hall, I had it all from Jessop and guessed where you would hole up. If you remember, we had occasion to use Betsy's cottage once before.' He stopped abruptly, as if he had said rather too much.

'For this sort of thing, do you mean, father?' Judith held out the paper that had been discovered in Mr Edgecombe's riding-coat.

'How did you come by that?' Quite undismayed by his anger, she told him. 'This is an old list. There's been no more of it since I left England. That's true, Edgecombe, is it not?'

'We — ell!' Mr Edgecombe looked vaguely disconcerted. 'It did seem a great waste to disband so profitable an organization.'

'You nodcock! With your father's part in it known after your disclosures, the Preventives could have taken you with the goods in your possession as they pleased.'

'Maybe, did they know about the Old Hall which, be sure, they did not,' retorted Mr Edgecombe. 'The game was worth the candle. I am not so beforehand with the world that I could forgo it completely.'

'You'll do it now!' Mr Hammerton was very emphatic.

'He certainly will do it now,' Euphrasia was no less firm, 'for I have no wish to wed a free-trader.'

'To wed — Euphrasia, have your wits gone begging?' Mr Edgecombe raised his eyes to Heaven in supplication. 'I'll not have a feather left to fly with!'

'Nor,' continued Euphrasia, very much in the grand manner, 'have I any desire to live on your ill-gotten monies. When I come of age we can manage very well upon my inheritance.'

Mr Edgecombe regarded her with affectionate amusement. 'And how far d'you think that would stretch?'

'Is not five thousand a year sufficient for our needs?' she asked in innocent wonderment.

'Five thousand — Euphrasia, you *must* be all about in your head!'

'No, dear Jasper,' she said, kissing him warmly on the undamaged side of his face, 'but I fear we must contain ourselves for the most of a year until I attain the age of twenty-one, because mama is unlikely to give her consent — unless, of course,' she suggested hopefully, 'you run off with me as you did with Judith.'

Mr Edgecombe implored her to try for a little conduct, to which remark she instantly took exception, pointing out that his own behaviour had hardly qualified him to criticize that of others.

'If you are lacking a house to live in, you are welcome to Netherdene with my blessing, Jasper,' said Rodney cordially.

'Now there is a back-handed turn if ever there was one!' complained Mr Edgecombe, assuming a nonchalant air to conceal his astonishment at the munificence of the gift. 'Well you know I've no love for the place.'

'We could always leave mama there and live in the Dower House,' Euphrasia was quick to point out.

There is no saying which way this argument might have gone had not the attention of the company been diverted by Miss Cartwright's demanding of Mr Hammerton when he was going to come to the nub of the matter.

'Aye, I had hoped to ease it along more gently,' he said, his eyes on Judith. 'Y'see, Georgiana and I were betrothed a few weeks back in Lisbon.'

'Then,' said Miss Routledge to whom this announcement came as no very great surprise, 'just who *was* in the secret passage that night I was locked into it? You, Miss Cartwright?'

''Twas I, ma'am,' admitted Mr Hammerton, 'and you very nearly caught me out. Had you traversed the passage beyond the stairway you must have discovered the door to the cellars open to your touch. And you, too, my lord, all but surprised me,' he added, flicking one of his piercing looks at Lord Penston. 'I was so overcome at having shot Quendon in error that I felt bound to discover for myself how he went on, but dared not make my presence generally known for fear of scaring off my quarry.'

His quarry, sitting close to Euphrasia, bestowed on him a mocking glance from his good eye, but vouchsafed no comment for Judith had stepped forward to offer her congratulations to her father and Miss Cartwright. This she did with a shy dignity that appealed to the sensibilities of all present.

'I cannot pretend that it is not something of a shock,' she confessed. 'But, with all my heart, I wish you both very happy.'

'Bless you, dear Judith!' Georgiana embraced her with a fervour born as much of relief as affection. 'You can have no notion of how much I longed to tell you, but your father would not have it until your own affairs were settled.'

'And you have no need to fear that your expectations will be affected adversely,' said Mr Hammerton, watching his daughter a trifle anxiously. 'Come what may.'

'Oh!' said Judith in a rather small voice. 'I had not thought of that!'

'No, well, indeed, why should you? But it does happen, lass, stands to reason.' Her embarrassed parent frowned at his mirth-convulsed lady. 'Georgy, take a damper!'

Judith's colour had rushed up again and she looked so confused that Miss Routledge longed to comfort her but found Lord Penston's hand on her arm and permitted herself to be drawn apart from the central group in the saloon.

'These family confidences are scarcely our affair,' he murmured in her ear, and deftly whisked her out of the room, across the hall and into the small drawing-room, where he closed the door and advanced upon her. 'As everyone appears to be arranging themselves very nicely, it occurs to me that we might well do the same.'

Miss Routledge endeavoured to recall all the tenets of her impeccable upbringing and failed completely to bring to mind a single one of them.

'I — I do not understand you, my lord,' she said in what she knew to be the most unconvincing manner. It certainly did not convince Lord Penston.

'Oh, yes, I think you do, my dear, my very dear Miss Patience!' He possessed himself of her hands and held them firmly. 'Will you do me the honour of becoming my wife?' His wife! When the most she could have hoped for was to be offered a carte blanche, discreetly arranged, so as to cause no distress to Rodney or Judith! 'I allow,' he went on, drawing her into his arms and kissing her very gently, 'that there are — in your view, at least — some insuperable obstacles to be surmounted. But I would point out to you,' he kissed her again, less gently, 'that Rodney is well qualified to take care of Miss Judith, George Hammerton you may safely leave in Miss Cartwright's care — and there's a comeabout that will set the gossips' tongues a-clacking for many a day! — and do not, I beg of you, require me to consider the plight of Mr Edgecombe and Miss Euphrasia, for I do not regard their case to be at all my concern. Nor am I disposed to wait until it shall please our young people to settle upon a wedding date for, depend upon it, Hammerton will wish his daughter to be married in prime style. They have all the time in the world whereas we, my love, have squandered too many years without each other.'

'Yes, well — my lord!' she managed to utter, a trifle wildly.

'You did say yes!' He had gathered her even more closely into his arms and was kissing her in such a manner as to send her head spinning like a top.

'Yes, but —' she protested when she was given leave to breathe.

'But what, my precious goose?'

'Our situations in life are so far apart, you have known me so short a time —' Unable to detail the many obstacles which she felt sure must stand in the way of their harmonious union, she raised her eyes to him in appeal so that he was obliged to give her further proof of his affection.

'What matter if it be two weeks, two days, or two hours?'

Miss Routledge found herself incapable of summoning up any objection to this argument and, nestling her head upon his shoulder, listened only to the very gratifying things he was whispering into her ear.

'I must warn you, however,' he said, 'that I am a pernickety fellow, full of undesirable bachelor habits, which may be not at all to your liking.'

'If you mean by that, things like attending race-meetings,' she countered with commendable gravity, 'then I must insist upon accompanying you.'

'You shall do so,' he promised her.

'Nor must I be restricted at all times to being driven by you or by a groom,' she insisted. 'I wish to set up my own carriage — a perch-phaeton, for preference.'

'*Not* a perch-phaeton, I think, it would not be becoming to your consequence and besides,' he added mischievously, 'it is by far too expensive!'

'I can see we are not going to deal together at all well if you are resolved on being such a nipcheese!' she chided him. He drew her back into his embrace, his expression suddenly grave.

'Ask for anything else you please, but I will not have you tipped out into the road again to the danger of your life. I loved you from that moment, I do believe, when I held you, like some broken flower, in my arms.'

'Bonnet all awry and covered in dust and scratches!' she supplemented, laughter dancing in her eyes to match the sparkle in his.

'Bonnet in the road!' he reminded her, then, very humbly, he said, 'I adore you, my Patience.'

Thus encouraged, Miss Routledge dared to slide her arms around his neck and plant a shy kiss on his cheek. In response he lifted her off her feet and seated himself in a deep armed chair with her comfortably settled upon his knee.

'My lord!' she made muffled protest. 'Should someone come in, what will they think?'

'They can think,' said he, leaving off making love to her for just so long as he needed to speak, 'whatever they choose. But if I have any knowledge of human nature, our friends are occupying themselves in like manner in other parts of the house.'

Which, regrettable though it may be to have to admit, was no less than the truth.

Masquerade
brings you
the age
of romance

It was a time of wicked conspiracies and
dastardly plots . . . of virtuous ladies
abducted by the all-powerful lords of
the nobility . . . vicious highwaymen and
scheming villains . . .

It was an age of threatening intrigue and
swashbuckling derring-do, when strength
and swordplay were all that counted, and
right and wrong were as nothing.

But, it was also a time of pure romance.

Don't miss these exciting Masquerade Historicals!

15. Prisoner of the Harem by Julia Herbert

Enslaved by a barbaric Algerian corsair, a young Englishwoman finds that, for her, life and love are never to be the same. A fascinating story of a romance impossibly conducted within the confines of a true prison—a harem!

16. The Queen's Captain by Margaret Hope

A most unusual and heartwarming love story unfolds against the bloody background of war. While the feared Spanish Armada threatens England's shores, young Beth Howard must fight her own personal, and seemingly impossible, battle....

17. Gambler's Prize by Valentina Luellen

A Mississippi riverboat gambler...and an innocent young beauty from one of New Orleans's finest families. The surprising consequences of their wild attraction for each other will intrigue you to the very last page!

18. The Damask Rose by Polly Meyrick

A vastly entertaining tale of an impoverished governess suddenly thrust into the teeming world of Regency London and thrown headfirst into the mad whirl of parties, balls...and love.

19. Joanna by Patricia Ormsby

In Regency London the vicious, rejected suitor of a spirited Irish girl threatens to ruin her reputation. And not only is her good name at stake but her very life, as well!

20. The Passionate Puritan by Belinda Grey

Her Puritan upbringing hadn't prepared her for this! Her hand in marriage virtually sold to an arrogant Royalist, Abigail finds her conscience at war with her traitorous heart.

21. The Crescent Moon by Shirley Grey

A fascinating tale of intrigue unfolds in the court of France's King Henri II, as a beautiful young gentlewoman battles tremendous odds to be with the man she loves.

29. Loom of Love by Belinda Grey

Her struggle for the oppressed worker of the early 1800s takes a courageous young woman to the Yorkshire moors…and to a disturbing confrontation with love. A compelling romance novel.

30. Hostage Most Royal by Margaret Hope

The famous Orient Express is the backdrop for this fascinating and unique tale of a beautiful princess who unwillingly falls victim to the charms of a peasant.

31. A Pride of MacDonalds by Valentina Luellen

The exciting and heart-rending story of a Scottish Romeo and Juliet, in which a pair of young lovers from warring clans fight for their right to happiness.

32. Wed for a Wager by Julia Murray

An unusual marriage, shocking and daring jewel thefts, and a bold kidnapping are the ingredients of this intriguing romantic novel, set in Regency England.

33. Bond-Woman by Julia Herbert

Shipped to the New World and sold as a slave to a wealthy and arrogant plantation owner, an innocent girl struggles to save all she has left—her pride.

34. The Countess by Valentina Luellen

A young countess becomes a pawn in the vicious struggle for the rule of Russia. Her only hope lies with an arrogant Cossack, but he puts loyalty to his country before all else.…

35. Sweet Wind of Morning by Belinda Grey

With the volatile Elizabeth Tudor on England's throne, certain things had to be kept secret—particularly a country girl's tempestuous marriage to one of the Queen's favorite courtiers!

These titles may be available at your local bookstore.